Without Room Service

Without Room Service

• • •

Jackie Granger

Copyright © 2017 Jackie Granger
All rights reserved.

ISBN-13: 9781543190342
ISBN-10: 1543190340
Library of Congress Control Number: 2017902659
CreateSpace Independent Publishing Platform
North Charleston, South Carolina

TO MY EIGHT GRANDCHILDREN

Never give up on your dreams, kids!

CHAPTER 1

• • •

EMILY AND JANICE WERE LOOKING out the window from their room at the Plaza Hotel across from Central Park in New York City. They had just finished breakfast, delivered via room service, and were still clad in their pajamas and luscious terry cloth robes courtesy of the Plaza.

It was the first week in April in New York and the day was perfect. The sun glistened off the windows of the tall, glass and steel buildings. Today New Yorkers could actually use the word *azure* to describe the color of the sky overhead. Yesterday's rain washed out all the soot and smog that usually blanketed the largest city in the United States. The branches on the trees in Central Park were coated in a velvety green hue of the buds as the leaves were getting ready to pop open.

Even though she'd known Emily forever, Janice couldn't resist saying, "Honest to goodness, Emily, I can't see how you cannot be enchanted by this city. Just look at all the hustle and bustle down there on the streets. It's so vibrant and alive." She made a sweeping arc across the window. "It's all here. There is nothing you can't see or eat or experience – ballet, opera, theater, museums, parks, shopping."

Unlike Janice, Emily was having trouble seeing the charm of the city. "Yeah, just look at the swarm of people. Janice, I'll give you one hundred dollars if you can walk in a straight line for at least fifty feet down there. You know you can't. You'll be dodging someone after taking two steps. No, sorry. I need to be in the outdoors – no people, no honking car horns, no plethora of yellow taxi cabs, just blue skies, clean air and birds chirping."

"That's here too," Janice shot back. "You can have the birds in Central Park."

Emily squinted her eyes and cocked her head to one side and looked over at her friend. "You know when I think about it, I don't understand how you and I have remained such good friends for all these years. All your vacations involve room service and big cities. Me? I can hardly wait to get out of here. It's so cramped. No matter what we do we're surrounded by people. It's a fight to walk down the street, to get a cab, to get on the subway. Ugh. Give me quiet. Give me serenity.

Janice chuckled. "Well, we're friends because, other than vacations, we share so many other things. Just because I don't think a vacation consists of running around in loincloth, howling at the moon and sucking on pinecones as pure bliss, doesn't mean everything about us is different. We have the same sense of humor. And, we care about each other."

"For the record, I don't run around in loincloth." Emily smiled at her friend. "And I only howled at the moon that one time. Now listen, kiddo. I have gone with you to London, Paris, Beijing, Buenos Aires, Rome, the Baltics and now New York, so for our next jaunt, you have to try one of my vacations in the wilderness, okay? Promise me you'll go camping with Peggy and me next October. We're planning to stay at Peggy's cabin in Western Montana."

Janice shook her head and smiled. "Oh, wait until I tell Amy about going camping with you. I can hear my daughter laughing now.

A sad look came over Emily's face. "Your daughter joins in and gets a kick out of everything you do, Janice. I wish I could share things with my daughter, Nancy, like you do with Amy."

Janice put her hand on her friend's arm. "Nancy cares, Emily. She just has so many things going on in her life right now." She needed to lighten things up and get Emily out of this down mode. "Now, as much as I'm going to regret this," Janice said, "a deal is a deal. Next October the three of us will go marching off into the hinterland never to be heard from again."

Janice's words seem to do the trick. "It will be fun. Trust me," Emily said walking to the bedroom. She stopped in the doorway and turned back toward her friend. "You know, I may prefer nature over big cities, but I'm not that dumb." She smiled and wiggled her eyebrows. "What time is our appointment at the spa?"

CHAPTER 2

• • •

It was the end of September in Montana. The slow, dog days of summer were over. The sky was a deep blue and the yellow and orange colors of the leaves on the trees were vibrant now. The crisp autumn air quickened a person's pace, a harbinger of things to come within the next two months as winter would come barreling down out of the Artic. But the woman in the psychologist's office paid no attention to the weather. Her feet were pressed against the floor. Her hands on the arms of the chair were balled into fists. With her jaw clamped shut, the tendons in her neck were as rigid as steel. She was so taut that her spine didn't even touch the back of the chair. Her icy glare zeroed in on the doctor sitting across from her. He had just checked his watch for the third time during their session.

After Dr. Thomas looked at his watch, he kept his head down while he rubbed his forehead with the fingers of both hands. "Nancy," he said slowly. He sounded exhausted. "Normally, I try to let my patients work through their issues themselves. I merely pose questions or ideas to stimulate their thinking process without injecting my personal views. But I'm going to make an exception in your case." His head came up and he looked directly at her. "I really don't think you need to add your mother's camping trip with her friends to your existing problems. In fact from the things you've told me about her, she sounds more than capable of taking care of herself."

Nancy slumped in her chair as his words registered. She fought to get herself under control after his remark. Now it was her turn to raise her head and look directly into his eyes. "She's always going off to god-knows where. I just don't have time to add her shenanigans to all the other things I have to worry about. Furthermore, she embarrasses me with the things she does. Don't you get it? My friends snicker behind my back at the stunts she pulls."

"Get new friends," was the doctor's retort.

Her body came out of the limp position. Her back straightened. Her chin went up and her eyes became tiny slits as she looked down her nose at the doctor. "I am the Chief Operating Officer of one of the largest corporations in the state of Montana. I have maintained an image of professionalism and intelligence throughout my career. My mother, on the other hand, likes to live in the damn woods, for heaven's sake. She and her friends are in their seventies! That's too old to be doing things like this. And . . . she marches in every screwball, left wing parade on the planet, attends local government meetings and writes letters to the editor. What do you mean I don't have to worry about her or be embarrassed by her?"

"Nancy, does your mother love you? If something happened to you, would she be there for you?" The doctor's questions were not accusatory. He wanted his patient to discover what was important and what was not.

The questions caused Nancy to take in a breath of air. Tears welled up in her eyes. She had to blink several times; because she knew without a doubt, the answer to both questions was "yes". Before she could formulate a response, the doctor announced that their time was up.

When she walked out of his office she felt drained. She so wanted him to agree with her about her mother's antics, but he didn't.

I need to have lunch with Amy to see what she thinks about our mothers' latest camping in the wilderness idiocy, and I definitely can't miss my yoga class tonight. Calm, I need calm.

• • •

Janice stared down in amazement at all the brand, new, camping clothes piled high on her bed. "I'm so glad you're here, Amy. I don't know the first thing about what to take on a camping trip. I can't believe Emily talked me into this and you agreed with her. Last

April when we were in New York, she wore me down, and like a dummy, I finally agreed to go with her and Peggy on one of their camping trips. Looking out the window of the Plaza that day, I thought October was so far away. I figured by the time it came, I would be able to think of something like a root canal or a rare tropical rash to get out of going with those two. But within a blink of an eye, here it is October already, and I can't think of a single excuse." She sighed as she looked down at the huge pile of clothing on her bed. "I'm seventy-two years old! In all these years, I have never been on a trip that doesn't involve hotels with a concierge and room service, for crying out loud."

Amy folded the last pair of woolen socks and added them to the pile. She smiled at her mother's remarks as she looked down at her. Actually, she had been looking down at her mother ever since she was fourteen years old. That's when the tall genes inherited from her father kicked in and she shot up to 5'10" while her mother remained steady at 5'5''. "Mom, you're going to love this trip. I envy you being in the outdoors, breathing in fresh crisp air, looking for comets at night. You're going to be so surprised at the fun you will have. However, I must say, the most fun I've had so far is shopping with you. I don't think the camping gear store has any inventory left."

"Are you kidding? I had to start from scratch. I never owned any *outdoorsie* clothes in my life. I'll tell you what's funny," Janice said looking down at the boots on her feet. "It's these boots! I look ridiculous wearing them. And, they're so heavy. Tell me again why I have to wear these every day until we leave."

"You have to break them in now so you don't get terrible blisters when you're at the cabin. One of the worst mistakes *Newbies* make is waiting until they're actually camping before putting on new boots. That's a sure way to be miserable within hours. It spoils the entire trip. And to tell you the truth, I think those boots look kind of cute with the Vera Wang outfit you have on." Both mother and daughter laughed as Janice did a little jig.

Janice's cell phone rang. Caller ID indicated it was from Emily. "Hello, is this Jane Goodall calling from the wild?" Janice asked when she answered.

"Yes, and am I speaking to the Queen in Windsor Castle?" Emily replied. "How's the packing going, Janice?"

Janice looked at the mound of clothes and gear on her bed. "Well thankfully, Amy is here to help me. I have to say the pile is getting bigger and bigger. But, being the seasoned traveler that I am, I know once I start rolling everything up, the things should fit into the large backpack I bought. Or rather the large backpack Amy made me buy. How about you? You all set to go?"

"Hah. Need you ask? Of course, I am. Oh, Janice, I'm so glad you finally agreed to take one of my vacations. I know you'll have a ton of memories to take home with you," Emily said.

"Yeah, that's what I'm afraid of." Janice chuckled.

"No, no, no. They will all be good memories. Peggy and I will see to that," Emily said. "Listen, I called to tell you that we'll pick you up for the airport around four thiry-ish on the fourteenth? And then off we go into the foothills of the Montana."

Janice snorted. "I know what you call foothills and what I call foothills are two totally different things. I get a nosebleed just standing on a ladder, and anything over twenty feet is a mountain to me."

Emily laughed. "Think of the foothills as staying at the Waldorf in the penthouse. Oh, Janice, I'm going to make a believer out of you yet. See you on the 14th."

After Janice hung up, her daughter Amy wasn't about to let her mother get out of her camping trip preparations. She folded the last pair of pants and put it on the pile waiting to be stuffed into the backpack. "Okay, now that we have everything together, let's start rolling and get things into your spiffy, new backpack."

When they were through, the bag looked enormous. But everything did fit in it. "I don't know about this," Janice said as she eyed the bulging bag. "It looks about the size of Wyoming, for goodness sake. And, it doesn't have wheels. Where are the wheels? I only know how to go on vacations where I pull my suitcase. I can't believe I'm going to have to carry that thing and on my back!" There was a pained look on her face as she looked across the bed at her daughter.

Amy was smiling as she hoisted the bag off the bed. "Come on, let's try it out. I'll help you get it on your back." When she got the straps over her mother's shoulders, Amy said "Okay, mom. Now I'm going to let go of the bag."

When the full weight of it was on her back, Janice shouted, "Are you kidding me?" She took several steps backwards and fell over onto the bed. Her arms and legs flapped around as she lay on top of the bag.

Amy burst out laughing. "You look like a giant sea turtle that's been flipped on its back." Her mother glared at her. She took her mother's hands and pulled her upright again. "Now just stand there, because I have one more thing you are going to have to carry." She had one arm out toward her mother in case she started to list to stern again and grabbed the rolled-up sleeping bag off the bed. She tucked it under her mother's right arm and patted her shoulder. "Okay, let's see if you can walk into the kitchen and back."

"I'm not going. Call Emily and tell her I've died," Janice said before she even tried to take one step with the monstrosity on her back, but then step-by-micro-step she turned toward the door to begin her trek to the kitchen. Amy hovered around her until she made it to the kitchen and back. She then had to help her mom get the backpack off.

Janice flopped down on the bed. "Honest to goodness, Amy. I don't think I can do this."

"You'll be fine, Mom. You're not going to be lugging this around every minute. According to Emily, once the driver let's you off, you'll only have to walk about a half a mile to reach the cabin." She watched as her mother's eyes shot open and her eyebrows got lost in her bangs. "Ah, then you'll unpack and won't have to carry it again until you leave," she added quickly.

Janice's upper lip curled into a snarl. She squinted her eyes at her daughter. "I'm going to write you out of the will for talking me into this."

• • •

Two Weeks Earlier
Oval Office of the White House

Trudy Hanson, the President's secretary, ushered the Vice President into the Oval Office. He was here for his 9:30 a.m. meeting with the President of the United States, Charles Mellon. This was the third year of their first term in Office. The President stood when Bill Andersen came into the Room. He waved his hand indicating the Vice President should take a seat across from his desk. "Morning, Bill. Have a seat."

"Mr. President," Bill nodded as he sat down.

The President smiled and shook his head at his number two-man. "You know, Bill, I sure wish you would call me Charlie.

We've been friends since our days in the Senate when you were Bill and I was Charlie. Nothing's changed except the address."

"I know," the Vice President smiled back. "But the address change is a big deal. Besides I like the formality."

"Well, I haven't been able to change you in the last three years, so I guess I need to be resigned to it. Listen, the reason I called you in here is because Patrick Webber contacted my Chief-of-Staff and wants to set up a meeting with you to discuss the possibility of getting the conservatives in Congress to bend a little and be more responsive to our ideas than they've been in the past."

The Vice President cocked an eyebrow. He looked skeptical. "Patrick Webber, the ultra-conservative and your arch enemy? Even though you're a Republican, he refused to contribute one dime to your campaign, because he thought you were too liberal always trying to work across the aisle in the Senate? Are you kidding? What's he up to?"

The President leaned back in his chair and put his hands in his pants pockets. "Yeah, he's got me wondering the same thing. But we've got to do something. This country is so torn apart ideologically. It can't go on." He shrugged his shoulders and cocked his head to one side when he looked across the desk at his Vice President. "So if he's offering an olive branch, the least we can do is listen to what he has to say."

Bill ran his hand over his face and looked out the window. "I don't know. I just don't trust the guy," he said slowly. "Do you really think he and his far-right honchos are ready to talk?" He looked back at the President.

"I'll tell you, Bill. Right now I'm open to hearing what he has to say. At least it will give us a better understanding of where they stand. By the way, he wants to fly you to a condo he has in Western Montana for a few days. He thinks going there will keep the reporters away and give the two of you a chance to talk and share ideas. Can you clear your calendar and be ready to leave on Wednesday the 16th?"

Bill chuckled. "I'm the Vice President, so I'm quite sure clearing my calendar won't be a problem. I'll have my secretary confirm the date. And then I'll need to have firmer details from Webber as to the time and the itinerary so I can give it to the Secret Service. I'll call him when I get back to my office. Perhaps he'll give me a hint about just what it is he wants to talk about." He put his hands on the arms of the chair and began to rise. "So is that it? Anything else we need to discuss?"

The President rose. "No, that's it, Bill. Keep me informed.

CHAPTER 3

• • •

NANCY WAS FINALLY ABLE TO schedule a lunch with Amy a few days before their mothers were set to go off on their camping trip. She rushed into the restaurant with her cell phone clutched in her hand. Amy was already seated at a table. Just as Nancy sat down, her phone rang. "Sorry I'm late," she said hurriedly as she took the call. After a brief conversation, she set the phone on vibrate and put it on the table, then she took a deep breath, blew it out and looked over at her friend. "I only have 45 minutes, but I wanted to talk to you about our mothers' camping trip. I think it's one of the dumbest . . ." Her phone buzzed. She stopped speaking and picked it up to view a text that just came in.

Amy had a slight smile on her face as she watched Nancy frantically trying to multi-task. As soon as she responded to the text and looked up, Amy jumped in while she had a chance before the next phone message interrupted them. "Why don't we order some lunch?" she asked calmly.

"Oh, yeah," Nancy said and glanced at her watch before picking up the menu. "I have to get back to work, so I'll have something simple that won't take too long to serve." Her phone jangled yet again. She answered the call. When she was through, Amy learned forward and looked directly into Nancy's eyes. "Put the phone away, Nancy. As you say, you'll only be here for 45 minutes. The world as we know it will not end in that short of a time."

Nancy's eyes widened and her jaw dropped. The very thought of turning her phone off made her panicky. "I can't do that, Amy. I'm in charge of many projects at work. I have to be available 24/7. And what if something happened to Scott or one of the boys and I couldn't be reached. Don't you worry about things like that?"

Amy smiled. "Okay, first of all, I care very much about my family. But I don't think in terms of *Oh my gosh! Something horrible is going to happen*. I couldn't go through life with those types of thoughts constantly in the forefront of my mind. So turning my phone to vibrate and keeping it in my purse while I'm having lunch with a friend, is no big deal to me." She raised her eyebrows and shrugged her shoulders in a questioningly look.

Nancy put her elbow on the table and rubbed her forehead. "My life is out of control, Amy. Everything is falling apart and no matter what I do, nothing seems to help. I'm spending such long hours at work that I'm missing my boys grow up. Scott is threatening me with divorce, because he feels I haven't got my priorities straight.

I'm seeing a psychologist who keeps looking at his watch during our sessions like I am just wasting his time. I . . ." She couldn't go on. If she did, she knew she would lose it completely.

"Hum," was Amy's response as she tried to sort out everything Nancy had thrown at her. "Well, let's take one thing at a time. I'm not a marriage counselor, but I am a professor in the MBA program. And watching you try to juggle everything just in the short time since you sat down, tells me you're right. Things are out of control in your life. So tell me a little bit about your job and why you think you have to spend so much time at work. Are you short staffed? How many projects are you in charge of? What are the people like who work for you – educated, qualified, dependable?"

Nancy shot out of her *woe is me* position and glared at Amy. "I wouldn't even think of hiring anyone who wasn't qualified. I have six people under me, and two major projects that need to be completed by the end of next month. And that doesn't count all the fires I have to put out on a daily basis. Now to top it all off, I have to worry about my crazy mother going off to god-knows-where." Nancy said.

"I teach a graduate class in management styles. And, yes, I do start some of my lectures with *'Now in the real world'*," Amy smiled and wiggled her eyebrows. "The most out of control manager is the one who micro-manages. The one who doesn't delegate and is constantly trying to take control of every single step in the process.

People under these types of managers are never free to create or to problem solve. And, watching how frantic you are right now, I think you're a micro-manager, Nancy."

Nancy's spine stiffened even more and her eyes squinted. "I am in charge of major projects. The buck stops at my desk. Of course, I have to keep on top of things. If I didn't, something might go wrong," she said.

"Well, here's another thing that gets lost under micro-managers," Amy said. "You lose the synergy of your group. The dynamics of individual groups is they take on their own identity and creativity, and when the only viewpoint allowed is that of the manager, the group identity and creativity goes right out the window. You just said your people are educated, qualified and dependable. That means, bottom line, they're more than capable of problem solving. So if problems arise, let your staff solve them. People as high up in the corporation as you shouldn't be putting out fires. That's the job of middle management. You guys are the strategic planners." She watched as Nancy made a face and rolled her eyes.

"I know I'm in my lecture mode," Amy said with a smile on her face. "It goes with the territory. But here's the corker, especially in your case. The reason you spend so much physical time at work and then continue to work while you're away from the office is because you are spinning your wheels doing more than one job. For you, Nancy, by micro managing you're not only doing your job, but you're also performing the jobs of the six people who report to you. No wonder you think your life is out of control. You're doing the work of seven people!"

Her jaw dropped open as she stared at Amy. "But if something goes wrong, I'm the one that has to answer for it."

Amy leaned across the table and laid her hand on Nancy's. "Trust those good people you've hired. Instead of hovering over them every single minute of every day, have them report to you on a weekly basis. If a problem should arise, they will have worked it through by the end of the week and will have answers for you."

"Oh, Amy. That's such a radical change for me. I don't think I would be able to sleep at night."

"Do you sleep now? Or do you toss and turn juggling the requirements of those seven jobs? When five o'clock at night comes, you need to go home and get to know your family again."

Nancy gave a stifled laugh. "You're right. But I don't know . . ."

Amy slowly shook her head at her friend. "Oh, Nancy. Look at yourself. Here you are sitting with a friend. We should be yakking away getting caught up on all the news. Instead you're going off in ten different directions answering phone calls and text messages leaving you little time to complete a single sentence. Put your phone away and let's talk. Now tell me why you're upset about our mothers camping trip."

The unhappy look on Nancy's face as she dropped her phone into her purse said it all. She hadn't been without a cell phone in her hand since the day they were invented. For a few moments she sat looking at her purse before she finally set it on the floor next to her chair. She looked up at Amy and scrunched her face. "What did you ask me again?"

Amy smiled. She knew how difficult this first step was for her friend. She also knew that Nancy was a major "control freak", but the wrong kind. If she could help her stop trying to control other people's lives, it would free her up to be in control of her own life. "Why are you upset about our mothers' camping trip?"

"Oh, right. Well, Amy, don't you see they're too old to be going off camping in the wild. Do you know my mother told me there isn't any phone connection in the cabin where they're staying? Good grief! What if something happens?"

Amy held up her index finger. "Ah, ah, ah," she warned Nancy with a smile. "Get rid of those thoughts. If something does happen, those three women have years of experience under their belts. There is very little the three of them haven't been through if something should arise. So stop worrying about their trip. Look at me. My zany mother has traveled all around the world, and I never hear a word from her from the day she leaves until the day she comes back home. In fact, I think in all her travels, I've received only one postcard and that arrived one week after she came home."

While they were eating, they continued to talk about their mothers' up and coming trip. Nancy in the hand wringing mode and Amy in they will have a blast mode. Over dessert, the two of them finally got caught up with each other and their kids. As they were paying the bill, Nancy glanced at her watch. "Oh, my god! We've been here for over an hour and a half!"

"Fun wasn't it?" There was a twinkle in Amy's eyes as she smiled at her friend. "Now before we go, I want you to try meeting with your staff only once a week. Tell them if problems come up, they have to solve them and give a report during the next weekly meeting. Come on – give it a shot. And, if you get through at least two full weeks of operating like that and everything works out, you have to promise to come and speak to my Graduate class about what you learned."

Nancy didn't move. She stared straight ahead. After a few moments, she moved only her eyes toward Amy and slowly let out a breath of air. "All right. I'll try. But when I speak to your class, I'm going to tell them you're really a kindergarten teacher who got lost on the way to work."

Amy laughed. "Fair enough."

CHAPTER 4

• • •

Janice was the last person to be picked up on Monday morning. Emily and Peggy arrived in her driveway at 4:20 a.m. It was still dark. In the middle of October the sun wouldn't be coming over the horizon for another three hours.

Peggy was sitting in the front seat in shotgun position. "I still can't believe you talked Janice into going camping with us," she said to Emily. "In all the years I've known her, she hasn't gone anywhere that doesn't have all the amenities." She started to chuckle. "This trip ought to be a real eye opener for her."

Emily had to smile at Peggy's observation. "But she is such fun to be with," she replied. "Even though she prefers her creature comforts, she's game for anything. Remember going down the bobsled run the Soviets used to practice on for the Winter Olympics when the three of us traveled in Latvia? That was Janice's idea."

Just then Janice came out her front door. She was dressed in brand new, unsoiled, outdoor clothing. Nothing looked washed out or faded. A few moments later, Amy came out of the house carrying her mom's backpack. It looked stuffed. She waved at Emily and Peggy before reaching back inside to bring out another suitcase.

Emily took in a quiet breath of air when she saw Amy here with her mother at four-thirty in the morning. Sadness washed over her. *Why couldn't Nancy be a part of this with me like Amy was? Why did she seem so disgusted when I tried to share this camping trip with her?* She was brought out of her musings when Peggy jumped out to help Janice with her gear. She also got out and opened the back of the van.

Janice seemed confused when she looked into the back. Even without Janice's gear, it was jam-packed. "There doesn't seem to be anymore room in there. What is all this stuff?"

"Don't worry. Everything will fit," Emily said. She moved one of the coolers sideways. "Actually, most of this is food and water. Peggy and I could live off the land, but since this is your first time, no sense in scaring you." She smiled and winked at Janice.

Peggy slid the side door open. "We'll shove those bags to the middle of the back seat so Janice can sit next to the window." She turned to Janice and with a straight face, she said, "If it's too snug back here, you can always roll down the window and lean out until we get to the airport."

"That's not even funny," Janice replied. "Wait. Amy wants to take a picture of the three of us before we leave, but we have to go back into the house where there's some light."

Once inside the three women stood together so Amy could take their picture. She looked at the three friends standing together. There stood her Mom with her dyed, blond hair. She traveled all around the world enjoying adventure after adventure, yet she would kill before she'd let anyone know she had even one grey hair on her head. Emily, ever the mediator was in the middle with her arms around her two friends. She did all the planning and always made sure everyone was taken care of. *Nancy you are missing so much fun. Why can't you see what a neat person your mother is?* Peggy, rounding out the trio, was the most down-to-earth person of the three, a very solid person who could always be counted on. *How lucky they are to have each other.* When the picture taking was over, everyone went back outside. The women got into the van.

After Emily started the engine, she announced the timeworn phrase that in all likelihood was even uttered by the Romans as they set out to conquer the Gauls, "And we're off." Amy waved as they pulled out of the driveway.

They made good time and arrived at the airport hangar at five o'clock on the dot, but they had so much luggage. It took them almost thirty minutes to unload and stow their gear into the single-engine plane. Even then, each of them had to carry a bag of food on their laps. The pilot was alone in the front of the plane while the ladies took the seats behind him. The plane taxied to the end of the runway. The pilot turned the nose of the plane facing north into the wind and revved the engines. As the plane gained speed going down the runway, the wings lifted slightly as the plane began to fly itself right before the actual liftoff.

Communication was almost impossible in the small plane because of the engine noise, so the women sat back and enjoyed the beautiful scenery below. In less than an hour they arrived at the Stevensville airport. A driver and van were waiting for them in the hangar. He would be driving them up to their cabin in the foothills. Now they had to reverse the procedure – unload the plane then reload the van.

Everyone thoroughly enjoyed the hour drive to the cabin. The yellow autumn leaves were still on many of the trees, and their color stood out against the green backdrop of the majestic pine trees. The sky was a deep blue. There was a reason why the state of Montana was known as the *Big Sky Country*. The foothills seemed to be just as awesome as their parent – the Rocky Mountains. Even Janice commented on the natural beauty of the landscape. "Quite a state we live in isn't it?" she said to no one in particular.

The van left the highway and proceeded on a dirt road. The ruts and potholes did not make that part of their journey very pleasant. When the van stopped, Janice looked around. She saw nothing but trees and rocks. "Where's our cabin?" she asked.

"Up there" the driver said pointing straight up.

"What do you mean up there? You have got to be kidding. How are we going to get all this stuff . . . up there?" Janice asked mimicking the driver by pointing to the top of the van roof.

"It's only about a half a mile to the cabin and we'll go slow," Emily added. When she got out of the van, she opened the side zipper of her backpack and took out two sets of small bells. The bells were attached to a ribbon with a clip on the top. Peggy was already attaching her bells onto the back of her jacket. Emily had a sheepish smile on her face as she looked over at Janice. "Turn around and I'll clip this on the back of your jacket."

"What is this all about," Janice asked in a very low and menacing voice.

"The bells are to keep bears away. We have to wear them whenever we go into the woods. The bears will stay away from us when they hear the bells." She decided not to tell Janice the bells also kept the cougars away. One thing at a time.

"You can't be serious?" Janice said to the two women.

"Oh, come on, Janice. You've lived in Montana all your life. You know we have bears up here." Peggy told her friend.

"What's that old Vaudeville line? 'All things considered, I'd rather be in Cleveland,'" Janice said.

They had to make four trips up and down the hills in order to get all their gear to the cabin. They started with the containers of food and ended with their backpacks and sleeping bags. Even the van driver pitched in and helped carry things. After the final trek, Janice collapsed on recliner in the cabin living room area and closed her eyes. "Wake me up when this vacation is over. I'm not moving until then."

After a short rest by all three women, Janice finally had a chance to look around and inspect the cabin. "This is fantastic, Peggy," she told her friend.

The structure was built out of huge logs. A porch ran along the entire front of it. The cabin was clean and well kept. Other than the bathroom in the back corner, the interior was comprised of one large rectangular room. Three bunk beds were lined up along the back wall. The front windows looked out at the forest and were covered in lace curtains. A sitting area with chairs, a sofa and rustic coffee table were arranged in front of a large fireplace. The kitchen was across the room from the fireplace. There was a dining area with a table that could seat six.

"There is an outside generator that provides the electricity and a well on the side of the cabin supplying water. Actually, this is a condo for lack of a better word," Peggy told Janice. "The developer built these cabins as rental property. But then he ran out of money and had to sell each of them off as condos. I come up here as often as I can and just love it, because it is so remote. It rejuvenates my soul. Each of the cabins is over one city block apart. Even in the tourist season, you don't even know anyone else is here."

Peggy started to open the coolers and sacks of food and began putting things into the cupboards and refrigerator. "I'll fix us some brunch. I'm starved. How do scrambled eggs, bacon and toast sound? I know it's a little late for breakfast, so let's just call this brunch." Janice and Emily nodded their heads in agreement.

Emily came into the kitchen area. "I'll start the coffee and pour the juice." Janice started to rise and offered her help. Emily said, "No, Janice. You just relax for now. You can be in charge of supper tonight."

Without uttering another word, Janice leaned back on the recliner with a smile on her face. "No argument from me. Good grief. If I can't even unpack a van without collapsing, how am I going to survive an entire week up here?"

"Not to worry," Peggy said. "The worst is over. The rest of the week will be pure enjoyment."

Janice turned her head, squinted and glared at Peggy out of the corner of her eye. She didn't believe her for a minute.

When the food was ready, the three of them came to the table. "Okay, ladies, we have to talk about what we're going to do today," Peggy said. "Because we've done so much lugging to get our stuff up here this morning, I thought we could relax and just go canoeing on the lake this afternoon. I keep the canoe in my shed behind the cabin. Then after we've had a good night's sleep and are rested, tomorrow we can spend the day hiking so Janice can get the lay of the land. It's just beautiful up here. How does that sound?"

"Sounds good to me," Emily said.

Janice took a sip of coffee. "Yeah, I'm game for canoeing now that I've had time to rest. But . . .ah . . .about tomorrow, just what does *hiking* mean to you two? Because to me hiking means once around the cabin and then we rest for the rest of the day."

Emily smiled. "Come on, Janice. You need an attitude adjustment here."

CHAPTER 5

• • •

After the breakfast dishes had been washed and wiped, they got dressed for their trip on the lake. It was mid-October up here in the foothills, which meant they donned their parkas, mittens, hats, scarves, long underwear, and wool socks. Winter would be setting in within a matter of weeks, and the wind blowing across the lake at this time of year could be quite brisk.

Peggy unlocked the door of the shed. The three-seat canoe was upside-down on sawhorses along the north side of the shed. Three sets of paddles and life vests were hanging on hooks above it. Peggy took the life vests down and handed them out. "We should put these on now. It will be one less thing we have to carry down to the lake." Then she turned to her friends. "Well, how do you want to do this?" She pointed down to the knee-high rubber boots she had on. " I'm wearing my rubber boots so I can stand in the lake and push us off. They're not the best boots for walking down the path to the lake. They don't grip the ground like your hiking boots do.

So why don't you two portage the canoe down and I'll guide you on the way." She reached over and gathered the six paddles. "I can take the paddles, then we'll be all set when we get down to the lake."

"Hold it," Janice announced. "What exactly do you mean by Emily and I will *portage* the canoe to the lake?"

Emily rolled her eyes and a look of skepticism ran across her face, because she knew what was coming once she and Peggy explained how they were going to get the canoe to the lake. She decided the best thing she could do was to act assertive with Janice or they'd be here all day arguing. She walked over to the canoe and with a sweep of her hand boldly said, "You and I are going to carry this down to the lake."

Janice's eyes popped open and her eyebrows shot up. "Now hold on a minute. You and I are going to carry that?" She pointed to the canoe. "It looks as long as an atomic submarine, for crying out loud." Her voice was one decibel below an all out shout.

"Calm down, Janice," Peggy said. "It's not that bad." No way was she going to tell her that she and Emily would be carrying the canoe on their shoulders with their heads *inside* the canoe. Let Emily be the bad guy on that one.

"Here's what you and I are going to do, Janice," Emily said. "We need to get this thing on our shoulders, and then we're going to carry it down to the lake. That's what Peggy means by portage. She'll walk beside us and guide us while we go down."

Janice stood there staring at Emily. Only sounds with esses and arrs and grrs came out of her mouth. Emily winched when one of those garbled noises sounded just like the word "shit".

Peggy tried to hide a smile. She didn't think this was the time to make fun of Janice. She walked over to the side of the canoe. "Come on, we'll show you what you have to do. You and Emily are going to get under the canoe and grab a hold of the seat," she said. To demonstrate she ducked under the front of the canoe and raised it a few inches off the sawhorses. She came back out and said, "You take the back seat Janice and Emily will take the front. I'll stay in the middle and help with the initial lift. When you have the canoe up on your shoulders, I'll guide you down. After that it's simple. You just carry it to the lake and put it in the water. *Voila*, we'll be ready to go."

To get the show on the road and to keep Janice from whining, Emily said, "We always do our final lift on three."

Janice did not say one word, but glared at her friends before she ducked under the canoe and positioned herself next to the back seat. On three, they all lifted the canoe on their shoulders, and Peggy step out.

"Oh, my God!" Janice yelled. "What are you doing? The canoe is covering our heads. I can't even see. This is nuts, Emily. We're never going to make it."

Since the canoe was made out of metal and their heads were completely inside of it, Janice's yelling was amplified. Emily thought her eardrums would burst as her friend's words caromed off the sides of the metal canoe.

Peggy learned under the canoe and faced Janice. "Stop yelling. You can do this, because I'm going to walk along side of you and talk you two down the path. Keep your eyes on the ground so you can see where you're walking."

Janice began uttering guttural sounds again. The other two were positive they heard the "s-h" word again.

Peggy guided them down with no major problems on the descent. Then she got under the middle of the canoe and told Janice how to get it off her shoulders and down on the ground. They used the count of three to lower it with Peggy assisting.

"The worst is over, Janice. Now the fun begins," Emily smiled.

"You know you two have been saying that to me all day – *the worst is over* – and then we seem to get involved in another horrible thing. I'm saying right here and now, this better be the last *the worst is over* I hear from you for the rest of this week, And you," she added as she rounded and glared at Emily with pure fury on her face "You talk about how hard it is to get around in New York. Hah! In the time it took to get this thing down here, we could have gone to the Met and been enjoying the second act of *La Boheme* by now. Peace and serenity of the great outdoors, my foot."

Emily put her arm around her friend. "It's not so bad, and once we're on the lake, it will be beautiful." Janice just snorted.

Peggy arranged two paddles next to each of the three seats. She pulled the canoe into shallow water with the tail still near the shore so that Emily and Janice could hop in without having to wade in the water. She told Janice to sit in the front, Emily to sit in the middle and she would get in the back seat. Once Janice and Emily were in and seated, she waded into the water and was able to push the canoe out into the lake so it would begin to float. She then jumped in the back seat.

At first Emily and Peggy used their paddles like gondola poles in order to get the canoe into deeper water. When they were floating freely, they had to teach Janice how to paddle. "You hold the paddle like this and bring it into the water and make a J," Emily said. She put her paddle in the water, pulled back so it was behind her, brought it out of the water and swung it to the side above the water to the front before putting it back in the water repeating the process a few times. It took Janice several tries before she got into the rhythm.

"You keep paddling on the left side, Janice," said Emily. "I'll paddle on the right and Peggy will just guide us." And off the three of them went.

It was so quiet on the lake. The cold water was very clear. The women kept their canoe along the shoreline rather than going out into the middle of the lake. Janice had calmed down somewhat and seemed to be enjoying the ride.

"How you doing up there, Jeanette MacDonald?" Emily asked.

Janice smiled and broke into a rendition of *Indian Love Call* in a falsetto soprano voice. *"When I'm calling you . . . oo . . .oo . . . oo. Will you answer too . . .oo . . . oo? Then I will know my love . . ."*

"Enough," Peggy called from the back. "You're scaring all the fish."

"I love that song," Janice shot back. "And this is the perfect place to sing it." She continued to hum the song as she paddled.

Up ahead the land jutted out into the lake. They had to paddle farther out in the lake to be able to make the turn. As they came around the outcrop, they spotted three bears standing in the shallow water along the shore.

"Oh, my God, bears!" Janice screamed. "Where are the bells? Start ringing the bells." She then began paddling furiously trying to get away from the bears up ahead. But the problem was she was paddling on the left side of the canoe. Doing that only made it go to the right toward the bears. Emily started paddling hard on the right side trying to counter act Janice's strokes.

"Stop paddling, Janice," she shouted as they continued to veer to the right. By now Janice was so out of control, her paddle was moving as fast as a piston in a race car engine going down the track at the Indianapolis 500.

Even with Peggy in the back trying to counterbalance on the right, the canoe kept listing to the right. "Hit her with your paddle," she shouted at Emily. "Get her to stop."

"I can't do that," Emily yelled back. All the shouting finally sunk in and Janice stopped. "But we have to get away from the bears," she said. She put her paddle in the water once again.

"Don't you dare do that, Janice," Emily warned her. "If you paddle one more time, I'm going to throw you out of this boat." Now that she and Peggy had command of the canoe again, they were able to steer it away from shore out into deeper water and away from the bears. However, the women had made such a racket yelling at one another that it scared the bears. They had left the water and were now scrambling toward the woods.

"Oh good grief," Janice said with her hand over her heart. "That scared the daylights out of me. Can we go back to the cabin now?"

"Are you kidding? We just got out here. Keep paddling . . . but gently," Emily replied as the canoe quietly moved through the water. "We'll stay a little farther from the shore. Will that make you more comfortable?"

The women continued their journey for the next hour. Very few clouds were in the sky, so the sunlight shimmered on the water. There was hardly any wind at all. It was so peaceful as they went along. They hardly talked as they made a trip across the lake and back down the other side. Even Janice had to admit it was an enjoyable afternoon. Once on shore again at their starting point, they reversed their procedure and brought the canoe back up to the shed while Janice mumbled under her breath during the entire ascent.

CHAPTER 6

• • •

When they got to the cabin all three of them found a comfortable chair and sat down to regroup and relax. Janice looked over at Emily and Peggy. "As soon as I get my strength back and I can do more than turn my head in order to speak, I'm going to prepare dinner tonight. I won't need your help. You two can have the night off."

Both Peggy and Emily started to protest. But Janice said, "No. I have something special planned. So as soon as we're all rested, you two go outside and enjoy the rest of the day while I get everything ready."

About a half hour later, Emily and Peggy were shooed outside. The sun set came quickly in this part of the country. As soon as the sun started over the mountains in the west, it was lost from view and there was almost no twilight. The light quickly receded even though it was barely four o'clock in the afternoon. Once the sun was gone, the air got colder, so the women had donned their parkas before they came outside. They sat on the steps with their hands in their pockets and were quiet just enjoying the peace of the wilderness.

After a few moments Peggy said, "Well, I think Janice finally started enjoying herself this afternoon."

Emily chuckled as she looked through the trees up at the sky to see if the stars were beginning to show. "Yeah, but I bet she never goes on another camping trip with us ever again."

Peggy smiled and nodded her head in agreement before she leaned back on the top step on her elbows and watched the night sky arrive. "Oh, look, there's the first star. Remember when we were kids? *Star light, star bright, first star I see tonight.*"

Emily also leaned back and quietly enjoyed the tranquility that could only be found in the wilderness away from the craziness of the cities - the people, the sounds, the glare of garish lights flashing and shining. Still staring up at the sky, she asked, "Do you believe there is life on other planets?"

"Hmm," Peggy said as she raised her eyes brows and cocked her head to one side. "You know when we were young actually even into my twenties, I would have said, 'No. We're the only ones here. There is no other life in the Universe.' Back then our telescopes, with such limited views of outer space, were all we had. Our religions were still what I call *old-country basic* meaning it was the religion our grandparents brought over with them when they came during the huge influx of Europeans at the turn of the last century. You know all the stringent rules, all the emphasis on being a sinner. God is in Heaven, the Devil in Hell. Man is the center of the universe; yada, yada, yada. But now with the Hubble Telescope and all the other gadgets we've put into space, we're learning the enormity of just what we're apart of. So now I have to answer your question with a yes. I do believe there is other life on other planets." Still leaning back, she turned her head toward Emily. "What about you? What do you believe?"

"I agree with you. I'll tell you when I look at those pictures the Hubble Telescope has sent back, I can't even wrap my arms around the vastness," Emily answered. "I have to tell you what my twelve-year-old grandson told me two weeks ago. I'm still thinking about it. Somehow we got into a lengthy discussion of outer space and astronomy, and he said, *'You know, Nana, all those books and movies about people being watched without their knowing about it? What if all of us here on Earth are really part of an experiment and are being watched by something out in the Universe?'* That young kid, I couldn't believe he said that. I still think about it."

"Maybe in his own way, he just described God," Peggy said softly.

Emily looked over at her friend. "Good grief," she whispered.

Just then the porch door opened and Janice called them to come in for dinner. When Emily and Peggy came into the cabin, they were surprised to see the table set with a linen tablecloth, cloth napkins and a wine glass at each place setting. They looked at each other and smiled at what was to come.

"Wow, Janice. This looks beautiful," Emily said. "Can we sit down or do you still have things to do?"

"Nope. Everything is ready. Come and sit." Janice was standing at the stove. When the two of them were seated, Janice asked if they were ready? Both of them nodded with enthusiasm as Janice took a chair and joined them.

Janice picked up her phone lying next to her plate and pretended to dial. Then she said, "Ring, ring, ring." She stood up and walked back to the stove and put the phone back to her ear. "Room service. How may I help you?" Back to the table she went and said into the phone, "Hello. This is Janice in the penthouse." She gave Emily and Peggy a wink. "I would like to order dinner for three. We'll have three garden salads and three cheese tortellini dinners with marinara sauce. Also please bring a bottle of red wine and a loaf of Italian bread. Oh, and chocolate cheesecake for dessert." By now Emily and Peggy were grinning broadly at their friend.

Janice went back to the stove and said, "Thank you. Your meal will be delivered shortly." She pretended to shut off her phone. She put a towel over her arm and brought a bottle of red wine to the table. "Good evening ladies," she said. She took a corkscrew out of her pocket with a flourish and uncorked the bottle. She then poured a small amount into Peggy's glass and waited for her to taste it and give her approval. Once she nodded yes, Janice filled the three glasses.

Janice raised her glass for a toast. "I figured this would be as close to my type of vacation as I'm going to get up here. So here's to laughter and friendship."

"To laughter and friendship," the other two said in unison.

"This is such a nice surprise, Janice," Emily said.

"I second that," Peggy chimed in.

Janice then served the rest of the meal.

While the women were finishing their desserts of chocolate cheesecake, Peggy told them where they would go hiking tomorrow. "We'll go up into the foothills above the lake. The view up there is unbelievable. We can sleep in and won't have to worry about getting up early. If we leave here around eight or nine, we'll have plenty of time to get in a good hike."

Janice looked across the table and squinted her eyes at the three women. "And just what does 'up in the foothills' really mean?" she asked.

"I don't know the elevation," Emily answered. "But it's not that high or difficult an assent." Janice rolled her eyes and looked skeptical.

"Come on, Janice. You were such a trooper today and admit it, we did have fun canoeing today. Tomorrow will be the same," Peggy added.

After the table was cleared and the dishes washed, Peggy started a fire in the fireplace. Because there was no phone connection in the cabin, each of the women had brought books to read. "What are you reading Emily?"

Emily scrunched up her face in embarrassment and chuckled. "I'm reading a dopey romance novel. That way I can put it down and remember right where I left off when I pick it up again in two months. These things are so simple minded."

"Have you noticed in romance novels, all the heroes are hunks with chiseled chins," Janice asked. "What the heck is a chiseled chin?"

"Beats me," Peggy said. "I've never met a man with one of those. A weak chin, a fat chin, a double chin, but never a chiseled chin." The three laughed. "What would you do if a hunk with a chiseled chin walk in the door right now?"

Janice looked to the side with her lips pursed and her eyes slightly closed. "Well, I don't think I would do anything . . . too much trouble. First of all I'd have to shave my legs." It took a moment for the other two to react. They were not expecting that remark, but when the humor of Janice's remark hit them, they chuckled.

"Yeah," Emily chimed in. "At my age I have to spread moisturizer on my face with a paint roller, so after the legs, I would have to lug out the bucket of extra-strength facial cream. You're right – too much trouble."

"Oh, and don't forget the chin hairs," Peggy said as she bared her teeth and held her thumb and forefinger together and made a quick pulling motion on her chin mimicking a tweezers."

"See what I mean?" Janice said as she grinned. "Too much trouble. Ah, men have it so easy. Slap on a little aftershave lotion, pop a manly pill and they're good to go." The three of them burst out in raucous laughter.

However, by nine-thirty the books were closed. The fresh air of the outdoors and the physical activities of the day had taken their toll. The women were ready to go to bed. Each of them donned their flannel pajamas and heavy cotton socks before climbing into the cots under the heavy quilts. Peggy had turned the heat down to 45 degrees and by morning the temperature in the cabin would hover around 50 degrees. Great sleeping weather with just your nose peeking out of the blanket, but not so much fun in the morning when you first got out of bed and had to get dressed and fed while the cabin heated back up. Tomorrow it would take the heater about 45 minutes to raise the temperature 5 degrees. Such was the life in the wilderness.

CHAPTER 7

• • •

AT 4:30 A.M. THE NEXT morning, the three women were still sound asleep in Montana. However, in Washington D. C. with the two-hour time difference, it was already 6:30 a. m. as the SUV containing the Vice-President, a driver and two Secret Service agents pulled into the corporate hangar on the perimeter of Dulles International Airport. None of the people in the vehicle were happy, because taking off from Dulles International instead of Reagan National meant they had to get up an hour earlier. Dulles airport was west of Washington, D. C. out in the boondocks of Virginia. Reagan Airport, on the other hand, was a mere thirty-minute drive south of the city.

The Vice President was not going to fly to Montana in the official Air Force Two, Patrick Webber tapped danced and convinced everyone that the Press would be alerted if they flew to Montana aboard Air Force Two. They wouldn't have the privacy they needed to get things done. It was better if everyone flew in Webber's corporate jet. The Secret Service detail thoroughly checked out the jet yesterday. And, that was the reason the Vice President and his detail were now heading to Dulles.

For being a billionaire, Patrick Webber could be one cheap bastard, fumed the Vice President since everyone knew the airport rental at Dulles was cheaper than Reagan. He and his detail had to get up at 4:30 this morning to be on time for the take-off. And if that wasn't enough, now they were going to be stuck on that plane for almost six hours in order to get to the western side of Montana. *Why Montana?* Certainly there were more than enough places closer to D.C. where they could have met. Bill Andersen remembered how Webber seemed to tap-dance once again as he gave the President the cock-and-bull story about how the Montana location would ensure the Press wouldn't get wind of the meeting. It would give them the uninterrupted privacy they needed to thoroughly discuss all the issues.

The ground crew in the hangar was very efficient and the corporate jet was airborne by 7:00 a.m. By 8:15 a.m. breakfast had been served and dishes removed. However coffee, tea and juice were still available at the back of the plane. The only thing the V.P. thought somewhat strange was the fact there was no Steward on-board. The co-pilot was the one who came back and served breakfast and cleaned up. When he was finished, he returned to the cockpit and assumed his duties up front.

After some small talk with Patrick that didn't amount to much, the Vice President tilted his chair back and closed his eyes. He hoped he would be able to get a few hours of sleep before they got to their destination. His Secret Service agents were sitting behind him working on the "Washington Post" crossword puzzle.

Patrick Webber tilted his chair back too, but it wasn't to sleep. He gazed out the small side window of the plane at the intermittent clouds below. They were white and fluffy like popcorn balls. The morning sun was shining on the tops and east sides of them. This late in the year at this latitude, the ominous, dark storm clouds of summer were gone. Soon to be replaced by the dark heavy clouds holding the winter snow. The plane was now somewhere over the mid-west part of the country, nothing much for a person to see down there except farm fields and an occasional cluster of houses indicating a small city. Not like the Northeast where looking down a traveler saw one huge sprawl of cities and suburbs one right after the other with little or no break between them.

Patrick's environment was the Northeast where the movers and shakers were. It was where the power of the country was located. By his thinking, he was one of the most powerful men in the United States today. And very shortly he intended to be *the* most powerful man in the U.S. He glanced across the aisle at Bill Andersen. As he looked at him, his eyelids lowered and a slight evil smile formed on his lips. He looked like a deadly cobra hiding under the brush slowly slithering toward it prey. *And you, my friend, are going to be my ticket to the top.*

He turned back and ran his hand over his lower jaw. He lowered his elbow on the armrest and thought about his life. His grade-school days were pure hell. He was a fat, pudgy kid with little athletic ability. He couldn't catch a ball, was always last in races, and couldn't defend himself when the bullies picked on him. They made fun of him, called him "Beach Ball" and a "Crybaby" while they were pushing and punching him on the playground or on the way home from school.

It wasn't until he was twelve years old that everything changed. He was sitting in his Sunday school class. They were studying the story of Judas and the thirty pieces of silver. The class was told how evil Judas was for doing this. The other kids agreed with their teacher. But to Patrick it was like an epiphany as he realized that people could be bought -— even to the point of selling out Jesus. From that day forward, he knew true power did not come and would never come on the football field or the basketball court. True power came from being wealthy and having enough money to buy people and make them do what you wanted. From that day forward he set out to do just that. If a bully teased him, he would use his lawn mowing money to buy a bigger bully to beat the crap out of the kid. It didn't take long before everyone left him alone.

He brought his grades up and was able to graduate from a prestigious east coast university. He started out on Wall Street in hedge funds that provided his first nest egg allowing him to buy a small company, dirt cheap, because it was in trouble. He made sweeping changes in personnel, not caring about the people or their families. As far as Patrick was concerned, it was precisely those people who caused the mess. He was able to sell it for a profit within a year and a half. He put half into investments and used the rest to buy his next company. Never losing sight of his agenda to become extremely wealthy. The money and his investments began to pile up.

He made only one monetarily unprofitable investment, but it brought him more satisfaction than his millions ever would. All during grade school his biggest tormentor was Dennis Turner, a dumb jock who had more muscle than brains. Through the years, Patrick kept track of Dennis. He was now the Operations Manager of a medium sized tool and die factory that sold its products to the automotive industry. Patrick bought the company for well over the equity price. The first thing he did was to summon Dennis to his office. The jerk didn't even remember who Patrick was. He told Dennis who he was right before he fired him. He remembered how shocked and confused Dennis was. He couldn't believe he was being fired.

"For god's sake whatever happened was twenty-five years ago!" Dennis blurted out. And then he made a fatal error as he was storming out of the office. "You are one vindictive bastard, Beach Ball," he said before slamming the door closed. Patrick had to sit there for 30 minutes trying to get himself under control, because what he really wanted to do was kill Dennis Turner for calling him *Beach Ball* again. But he got his ultimate revenge. He continued to monitor Dennis. Every time he got a new job, Patrick made sure the owners would hear either by innuendo or through the grape vine slurs about Dennis until he was fired from yet another position. After a number of years, he was no longer interested in Dennis figuring he was probably flipping hamburgers somewhere. Other people who had slighted Patrick along way began to replace Dennis on his revenge list.

All the while he was climbing to the top of the most-wealthy chart, the greed of people never let him down. He had yet to meet one person who could not be bought. Sometimes the person would demand a large amount of money, but for the most part the majority could be bought for chump change. Politicians, prostitutes, executive business people, it made no difference. The common denominator was always that thirty pieces of silver.

The evil smile and the reptilian eyes returned. He looked over at the Vice President. *And won't you be surprised to learn who sold their soul on this plane when we land in four hours?*

CHAPTER 8

• • •

Peggy came awake slowly that morning. It was quiet. The other two women were still asleep. The sun hadn't come over the horizon yet, but the sky had begun to lighten so she was able to see inside the cabin when she opened her eyes and stared up at the ceiling. It was so comfy and warm under the puffy and soft quilt. She wanted to stay and enjoy the warmth, because she knew the shock of cold air would hit her as soon as she threw back the covers. However, in all fairness to the others, she knew she had to get up and crank the thermostat to get the heat going. She counted to three, drew the covers back and scurried to the thermostat across the room. Once done her feet moved even faster on her way back to the bed. She was shivering even when she was back under the blankets. *Poor Janice. This is going to be another shocker for her.*

Five minutes later Emily and Janice began to stir. As Peggy predicted Janice did not remain silent about how cold it was in the cabin. However, thirty minutes later all of them were up and sitting at the table. Emily had made coffee and filled each of their cups. Then each was assigned a breakfast task. Janice set the table and poured the juice. Peggy began cooking the eggs and bacon and Janice was in charge of the toast. Once they were seated again and enjoying the morning meal, they needed to decide their itinerary of the day.

"I think we should plan on spending all day hiking," Emily said.

Janice slumped in her chair, head hanging down, shoulders rounded.

Emily shook her head and smiled at her friend. "It won't be as bad as you think, Janice."

"No. It will probably be worse," Janice mumbled still remaining in her defeatist mode.

"No, no, no," Emily said. "We'll fill our pockets with snacks and bottles of water. We'll be stopping several times to rest and have snacks, so it will just be an enjoyable walk."

"One thing I know is we have to layer ourselves so we can remove clothing as we warm up while walking," Peggy added. "That means turtleneck shirt, sweater, vest and then parka."

Janice just looked at the two of them with her upper lip in a snarl. It was evident this was not going to be her favorite day.

After dishes were washed and put away, the women got dressed and started on their hike. Their pockets were full of fruit, snacks and water bottles. With all the layers of clothing and pockets bulging, they looked like each of them tipped the scales at over 300 pounds. The air was crisp but by now the sun was shining. It promised to be a grand day for hiking.

"Let's head north," Peggy said. "I want to go past a few of the cabins so you can see where they are. Right now it seems like we're isolated, but we're really not. Be interesting to see who else is in the other cabins." They started up the walking path in front of the cabin. At the top of small rise, they could see the roof of another cabin on the other side. "See I told you these cabins are about one city block apart."

"Doesn't look like anyone is in this one," Emily said as they came down the hill. The cabin was the same as theirs – made out of logs, porch along the front, and a storage shed in the back. They continued on the northern path through the woods, and after walking approximately another city block, they came up a hill where another cabin sat over the rise. This one didn't appear to be occupied either. It had the same layout as theirs, except this one had large dishes and electronic gizmos on the roof.

"Those things are new," Peggy said as she studied the roof. "I'll bet they were installed so the owners would have Wi-Fi. Interesting. Well, this is the end of the series of cabins that were turned into condos. I guess we really are the only ones up here. I'm surprised. I thought for sure there would be other campers around. It's not that late in the season either. As I remember it, the path behind this cabin is going to turn to the west and we're going to start going up. How you doing Janice? Can we keep going for a while?"

"I'm holding my own," Janice replied. "Actually, I'm imagining I'm on my way to Bloomingdale's. It helps me put one foot in front of the other." The two women smiled. Janice did not.

They passed the last cabin and turned to the west and then continued to climb. It took them an hour to reach the top of the first foothill. "I think we should stop here for a break," Emily said. All agreed, even Peggy. They each found a rock to sit on. The vista in front of them opened up so they could look down and see the entire lake. It was breathtaking. There was very little wind, so the sun shining on the surface of the water made it look like glass.

Emily pointed to the eagle silently approaching the lake. Because it was gliding down, its wing-span from tip to tip must have been five or six feet. "Watch," she told the others. "He's going to catch a fish." Sure enough, as it skimmed the water, his feet dipped in then up he flew with a large fish tightly grasped in his talons.

"Wow," Janice said. "I hate to admit it, but the hike up here was worth it."

Once they were rested, it had warmed up and they were able to remove their parkas. They tied the arms around their waists and started out again. They turned to the northwest and began to climb even higher. The banter they shared earlier in the day ended, since they were now involved in some serious hiking which needed all their strength. But the higher they went, the farther they could see. And the sights were astounding.

When they stopped to rest again, Peggy looked out in awe at the Rocky Mountains soaring thousands and thousands of feet above sea level looming in the distance beyond the foothills. The mountains above the tree line were beginning to be covered in snow. The granite rock making up the mountains here in the United States remained spiked and jagged along the top indicating they were still new mountains, unlike the much older Smokey Mountains on the East Coast. Those mountains were rounded and smooth having been subjected to wind and erosion long before the Rockies were formed. One hundred and eighty million years ago, the Oceanic Pacific Plate met the North American Plate and took a nosedive down into the Earth. For some reason, the Oceanic Pacific Plate then made an upward turn as the momentum continued to push eastward. It continued to travel straight under the Continent. The pressure of the Plate created such an unbelievable force that it pushed the granite upward from the bowels of the Planet to form an entire range of mountains.

Peggy was mesmerized by their grandeur. How loud was the sound of the screeching and groaning of the granite grinding and sliding its way out of the Earth as it continued its journey high into the sky, she asked herself. In the 1950's schools were closed for the morning, so the nation could stay home and watch T.V. to see the atomic bomb detonated in the Nevada desert. She remembered her mother cried as they watched the force of the explosion. Yet as horrendous as the atomic bomb was, that explosion was so puny compared to the force generated to create these mountains. Today the Rockies stand majestically and oh so quietly over the land without a hint of its monumental beginnings.

"You know, every time I see the Rockies, I think about the pioneers who came across this country in covered wagons. What was it like for them to reach a summit of one mountain only to see the next mountain they would have to cross? How many of them gave up?" she asked Emily and Janice.

"You're right," Janice said. "Today we gripe when getting somewhere by car takes more than an hour. Those pioneers opened our country."

"I think even I would have decided to quit after going over the second mountain and seeing the third one staring me in the face," Emily said. Peggy and Janice were surprised at what she said.

"What do you mean you'd quit?" Janice asked. "You who thinks the great outdoors is as close to heaven as a person can get. You've always been so adventuresome. You surprise me."

"Well, I do love camping and being in the wilderness. But if you'll notice, even if I stay in a tent, I always bring all the creature comforts with me – enough food and water and warm clothes. And I've never walked to a campsite. I've always gotten as close as I can to it by car first. So the idea of trudging up and down huge mountains in a wagon worrying about running out of food or whether the horses were going to die pulling the wagon up another mountain would make me quit and put down roots at the bottom of the second mountain."

"Well," Janice said. "You learn something new every day."

The three women decided it was time to move on. They stood and continued hiking to the west. The path began to bend to the south and they proceeded hiking down the foothill into the forest again. Suddenly a twin-engine plane flew very low directly above them. It seemed to be slowing down.

"Oh, my gosh," Janice said. "I think it's going to crash it's flying so low." They waited in agony for the explosion as they heard the plane fly even lower off to the south. Soon the sounds changed and they heard revving of engines as if the plane had landed and was taxiing down a runway.

"How can a plane land up here?" Peggy asked. "There's no runway that I know of around here." The women picked up the pace to see what happened to that plane. After about a quarter of a mile the terrain changed. They climbed up another hill and looked down into the valley. There below them was a man-made runway. Trees and forest growth for about two hundred feet on either side of the runway had been stripped away. The runway itself looked like it had been covered with asphalt. It had to be at least 5,000 feet long. The twin-engine plane was parked at the far end of the runway. By the time the women got there, the engines had been turned off. They could see a number of people moving about in the plane. No one seemed to be hurt.

"A stinking runway!" Peggy hissed. "How did that get here? Who built it? And why?"

"It looks like it's been built for access to the cabins," Emily said. "How stupid can you get?'

"Yeah, look at how much land had to be cleared even for that small runway," Peggy said. "It's got to be thousands and thousands of feet long. How many trees had to be cut down so a few rich people could land their planes up here. How many animals lost their habitat by stripping this land?"

"How much money was paid out to government officials to keep quiet about it?" Janice asked. Both women nodded their heads in agreement. "You know, I may like to travel to big cities, but that doesn't preclude me from being concerned about saving the wildness from destruction. All runways have to be approved before they can be built. And by law the plans have to be published before construction can begin. It gives people a chance to have their say about the proposal." Janice turned and asked Peggy, "Did you ever hear anything about this airstrip being built?"

Peggy had such a sad look on her face. "No, I never heard a thing," she answered her friend. "All this destruction for only a few people. It makes me sick. Every time the wilderness is destroyed, it is a big deal. We have to protect this planet for our grandchildren and great grandchildren. And if we don't do it, who will?"

They watched as three men got out of the plane. Even from up here, two of them looked huge. "What's with the two steroids," Emily asked.

"They don't look like campers to me. Well, there's nothing we can do and standing here staring down there isn't going to change anything," Peggy said. "Let's get on with our hike."

The women turned and retraced their steps down the small hill until they came to the path they had been hiking on. After 10 minutes another plane flew low overhead. But this plane was a small jet. Emily shielded her eyes from the sun high in the sky as she watched it descend. "That looks like a corporate jet. I wonder what's going on. Maybe we'll have some neighbors now," she said.

"Maybe the two beef-cakes are here to help unload the jet and carry the gear for the big shots. You've got to be kidding." Peggy said with a sneer on her face.

Emily checked her watch. They had been resting and hiking for over three hours. "If no one has any objections, let's start back to the cabin. Once the sun goes down over the Rockies, it gets dark in a hurry. If we start back now, we should have sunlight the whole way back." They agreed and decided to head back. By now the sun had reached its peak of warming the day, and they were able to unzip their vests. They were hiking at a leisurely pace now because they were going down from the foothills.

CHAPTER 9

• • •

As the corporate jet was landing, Patrick Webber looked out the side window checking to make sure the other plane had landed. It had. *And now it begins.* The sickening smile slide across his face again.

When the plane came to a stop, the pilot stayed in his seat to perform the steps of shutting down the plane. The co-pilot came to the rear of the plane and opened the exit door and let down the steps. The passengers began to unbuckle the seatbelts. Even though this was a well-equipped jet, it wasn't high enough for the men to stand erect. Once out of their seats, they had to duck down as they walked to the door. Six hours of sitting in the plane caused all of them to stretch and rotate their shoulders once they were on the tarmac.

The Vice President was surprised when two large men rounded the tail of the jet walking toward them. Agent Phil Daniels immediately stepped in front of the Vice President and kept his eye on the men as they approached. Breaking all protocol the other Secret Service man, Agent Jim Kovac, did not react, but remained standing next to Patrick Webber. With years of training and experience, Daniels assessed the situation and in an instant knew something was very wrong. His partner should have reacted in the same manner as he did to protect the Vice President. He reached into the side of his jacket, flipped the strap on his holster and put his hand on his gun. Without taking his eyes off the men he said, "Kovac, what's going on here?"

Agent Kovac had his gun out and pointed at his partner. "I wouldn't do that if I were you, Phil. Take your hand away from your gun."

Bill Andersen had been a Marine and served during the Gulf War in Iraq. He had been involved in a number of tense situations when he was on patrol over there. He too was able to assess the situation. Although he was stunned by the fact Agent Kovac was holding a gun on them, he was more concerned about the two strangers. They were all muscle like over-grown body builders. "What the hell is going on, Patrick?" he demanded.

Patrick stepped forward and looked at Bill Andersen. There was a smirk on his face. One eyebrow was raised. "Quite simply, Bill, you're being kidnapped."

Those three words, *you're being kidnapped*, had the effect of a sledge hammer. The Vice President's head snapped up, and he had to take a step back. "Are you insane?"

Patrick Webber's entire demeanor changed in an instant. His face shut down, but his eyes bore into the Vice President with absolute hatred.

Agent Daniels stepped closer to the Vice President and again went for his gun. The two goons reacted swiftly. One man grabbed him and held him by the arm, and the other man pulled his right arm up and retrieved his gun. Then, almost like it was choreographed, one held him securely from behind while the second one punched him first in the stomach and then in the jaw. The one-two punch was over in a matter of seconds.

"I told you not to do that, Phil," Kovac said quietly. There was no inflection in his voice. He then walked over, took a firm grip on the Vice President's arm, and led him over to Patrick Webber. At this point, Daniels wasn't in a position to protect the Vice President. He was still trying to catch his breath and was now spitting up blood from the sock to his jaw.

The Vice President looked over at Jim. "For god's sake, Kovac. How could you let this happen? He's your friend." The Agent showed no emotion. There was no look of guilt on his face as he stared over at his partner.

"Money, Bill. Everyone has a price even Secret Service agents," Patrick sneered. He turned to Kovac. "Get him back into the plane," he nodded in the direction of Phil. These men will guard the Vice President while you get things settled in the plane. The men took Daniels' arms and jerked him toward the open door. He started to twist and resist.

Before Jim could get near Phil to help subdue him, the Vice President called out, "Just do what they say, Agent Daniels. I'll be okay." He nodded several times at his Secret Service agent trying to reassure him.

After getting Phil settled in the jet, Kovac stepped down from the plane. He still had the gun in his hand. When he walked over to the Vice President, he shoved it into his ribs. "Daniels is going to remain on the plane and report in to the White House from here. But don't plan on Daniels uttering any coded messages for help. I told the pilots what all the emergency code words were. If he tries to use even one of those when he reports in, they have instructions to shoot him."

Patrick Webber told the two goons to go and get the pilot out of the twin-engine plane. He wanted him to go with them to the cabin.

Bill Andersen watch the men yank the pilot out of the other plane and down the stairs. "What the hell is going on?" the pilot shouted as they dragged him over.

Bill Andersen turned his head toward Patrick Webber. "Now what?" he asked with pure loathing.

"Now we go to the cabin and I'll explain everything."

CHAPTER 10

• • •

AFTER THEIR HIKE BACK DOWN the foothills, the women past the farthest cabin they had passed earlier in the day and were now walking on the path in front and were about to come up to the cabin next to theirs. When they rounded a slight bend, they were met by a group of six men. The two large men appeared to be from the twin-engine plane they had seen land earlier. Along with carrying some luggage, they were surrounding a smaller man. One of the steroids had a tight grip on man's arm. Three other men were behind them. The man on the left was dressed in expensive outdoor clothing. The man on the right was in a suit. He was holding arm of the man in the middle of the two.

Emily smiled at them. "Hello," she said. None of the steroids smiled back. In fact they edged closer to the man they were holding and pulled him closer. She got a chance to get a better look at the men behind them and was startled. "Good grief. You're Vice President Andersen," she said as she put her hand out to shake his hand. One of the steroids quickly moved to block her from touching the Vice President. She dropped her arm and took a step back. She was so rattled by the man's rude behavior.

The well-dressed man moved forward. "The Vice President is up here on a short camping trip." There was a smile on his lips but not in his eyes as he tried to defuse the situation. "Where are you ladies staying? Are you in one of these cabins?"

"No. We're staying at the lodge on the shore of the lake," Janice blurted out before the other two ladies had a chance to respond. "Well, it was nice to meet you, Mr. Vice President," she nodded to him as she began to walk around the group of strange people. It wasn't easy, since they took up most of the space on the path. "Come on, ladies," she raised her arm in a forward motion. "If we don't get back to the lodge soon, you know how our children worry about us. It wouldn't surprise me if they sent out a search party looking for us."

It took a few seconds for the Peggy and Emily to react and begin to follow Janice. Emily brought up the rear. Her eyes were squinted and there was a questioning smile on her face as she passed the Vice President. She gave him a slight nod as she passed.

As soon as they were farther down the path, Peggy whispered to Janice. "What was all that about staying at the lodge along the lake business? And why did you suddenly seem to want to get away from them?"

"Something is wrong,' Janice hissed. "Didn't you feel it? I just thought it would be prudent not to mention where we're staying." She put her finger to her lips indicating they should stop talking. The leaves from the foliage and deciduous trees along the path had fallen and were beginning to dry and turn brown. They made a crunching sound as the ladies were walking. Janice could hear the same sound behind them.

"I think we're being followed," she whispered. "I'm going to stop and tie my shoe. When I do, look back and check to see if you can spot someone." She stopped and bent down. The other two quickly spun around and looked behind them. Sure enough, one of the steroids tried to duck behind a bush, but not before they spotted him.

"Are you kidding me?" Emily asked. There was panic in her voice.

"Nuts to this," Peggy snorted. She had been coming up here for over ten years and never once had a bit of trouble. "Watch this." She turned around and marched back to where the man was standing behind the bush. Her back was straight and her chin up. There was a no nonsense look on her face. "Are you following us?" she asked the man. Even with his size he was looming over her, but she did not back down. She squinted and continued to stare directly into his eyes.

At first the man couldn't answer her. He shook his head as if he were trying to clear his thoughts. He seemed confused. "Ah, ah, no. I'm looking for something."

"What is it? Maybe we can help you find it," Peggy asked without softening her look or her stance. By this time the other two women had come over. Now the three of them surrounded him. He became even more agitated.

"Ah . . . a phone. One of the men lost a phone."

"What color was it?"

"Where does the man think he lost it?"

"Where are you going? We can go with you as you retrace your steps." The three women wouldn't back down.

He seemed to give up. "I'll try later," he said backing up on the path. "Maybe the guy just put it in a different pocket."

The three of them stood there and watched the man walk away. As soon as he was out of hearing range, Janice whispered to her friends. "I think we really shook him up,"

"Yeah, with his size, I bet no one has ever challenged him before," Peggy said in agreement. "He didn't know how to act."

"Nah," Emily added. "He just looked scared, because I think we reminded him of his mother." The other two women smirked at that idea.

The women decided they needed to put some distance between all those men and themselves. They turned and proceeded to walk towards their cabin. After several steps, Janice asked, "Why the heck were we followed in the first place? And when we first ran into those men, did you see the look on the Vice President's face?

He looked terrified. The guy in the suit looked like a Secret Service agent, but those other two gorillas sure didn't. And who was the man those two were holding on to?"

"You're right, Janice. Something is going on and it doesn't look good," Emily said. Just then she snapped her fingers. "Ah hah. I know who that other guy was, the one with the expensive outdoor clothes who asked us where we were staying. That's Patrick Webber. He has more money than God and is always giving money to beef up conservative political parties. It's like he is trying to control them. What is that creep doing with the Vice President? Same party as the Vice President, but our President and Vice President are more liberal and middle of the road than that Webber idiot."

When they reached their cabin, Peggy grabbed the women's arms so they couldn't turn toward it. "I think it would be better if we didn't turn in to our cabin right now. We're going to walk a little farther and then we'll look back to see if that guy is still following us." Mid way between their cabin and the next one, Peggy said, "Now." All three whirled around, but the path was empty.

"Come on. We're going to turn in here," Peggy said. "We'll back track to my cabin from behind. Just to be sure." As she started off the small bells on the hem of her jacket began to tinkle. She had been so upset about being followed she hadn't paid any attention to the bells. She reached behind her and tried to take them off. "Oh, these damn bells. We can't try to sneak around wearing these. They'll hear us wherever we go. Here get mine off and then I'll take yours off. We'll put them in our pockets. If we meet any bears, we give them a dirty look and scare the crap out of them. Come on we've got to hurry."

There was no path. They had to forage their way through foot-high ground plants and bushes. After 10 minutes of trekking through the wild, they reached the back of Peggy's shed. They stopped and leaned against it. Afraid to even peek around the corner in case the man was there and would spot them.

"We've got to go back and see what those guys are up to," Emily whispered. "We've got to see what's going on." The other two women took in a breath of air when they heard that. Frown lines appeared on Janice's forehead. Peggy bit her lower lip.

"I'm not kidding. The President looked terrified." Emily snapped. She peeked around the corner of the shed. "I can't see anyone. Come on. We'll sneak up to the side of the house." With that she started running toward the cabin.

The other two women shrugged their shoulders and looked at each other. "Might as well follow her," Peggy mumbled as she too took off. Janice wasn't far behind.

They stayed silent along the side of the cabin listening for the tell-tale sign of leaves crunching. Other then their own panting, they heard nothing. This time Peggy peeked around the corner of the cabin and watched for a few moments. Nothing stirred. "Now what?" she asked as she stood back against the wall.

"We've got to find out what's happening. You know that," Emily said.

"This is nuts. What if they spot us snooping around? We're just three old ladies against all those men," Peggy argued.

Janice was quiet and had her head down. She licked her lips and looked up. "Emily is right. We at least have to see what's up." Peggy opened her mouth to protest, but Janice held up her hand. "This is the Vice President of the United States. We have to at least make sure he's okay."

"All right, let's get this over with," Peggy said while slowly shaking her head. She made one more peak around the corner and said, "Okay. Let's go back and see what's going on over there."

Once they were on the path in front of their cabin, the women went as quietly and as quickly as they could back to the other cabin, however, now they concentrated on trying to only step on wet not dry leaves as they scurried along. When they came to the small hill before the last cabin, they stopped. They could hear voices on the other side. The voices didn't sound friendly. Slowly they shimmied up the hill and surreptitiously peeked over the crest. Ahead they saw the two big guys pushing and shoving the Vice President along toward the shed in the back. One of them also had a hold of the other man they saw when they first met the group of men, but now it looked like the man had been beaten. There was blood on his face and he stumbled as he was being pulled along. The Vice President said something, and one of the captors slapped him across the face. His head flew to the side from the force. Janice and Emily sucked in a breath of air. Peggy laid a hand on each of their arms then whispered, "Shhh."

The captors pushed the two men through the door of the shed. The women couldn't see what was happening inside. But they did hear a loud moan shortly before the two thugs came back out the door. They slammed it shut, and attached a lock on the handle before they walked back to the cabin and went inside.

The three women ducked back down on the hillside, and for a moment they just sat there stunned. "What the hell was that?" Emily whispered.

"Let's get out of here," Janice whispered. "We'll talk when we get away from here." Again, they tried to make as little noise as possible as they hurried on the path back to their cabin.

Once they were passed the next cabin, Janice stopped. "I think the Vice President has been kidnapped. What are we going to do? We've got to get help."

"We need to get back to our cabin and make plans about how we're going to do that," Emily said still in a whispered voice.

CHAPTER 11

• • •

ONCE IN THE CABIN THEY sat at the kitchen table. No one said anything. Each was lost in her own thoughts of the enormity of what they had just witnessed. None of them had any background to know what to do.

Peggy looked at her two friends. "Well, I think we need to call the White House and tell them what's going on. They're trained and will know exactly how to handle this. I'm sure they'll send in the military who are much better equipped to deal with this than we are."

Emily shook her head. "Just how does one *call the White House?* First, are any of our cell phones even charged up so we can make a call?" Peggy and Janice had a guilty look on their faces as they realized they hadn't even taken their phones out of their backpacks since arriving two days ago. Besides there was no reason to keep the phones charged, because there was no phone connection in the cabin. They had to go down to the shore of the lake to pick up a connection.

Peggy looked across the table at her friends. "So first we need to charge our phones and then we have to go down to the lake to be in phone range. In fact, it might be a good idea to plug our phones in right now to charge them up." All three women went to their backpacks and retrieved their phones.

"Oh rats," Janice said while she dug through her backpack. "I brought my phone, but I forgot the charger." She heard Emily and Peggy groan. "Hey, don't blame me. There were so many new things I had to pack for this trip. In the confusion of making sure I had all the camping stuff, I didn't even think about my phone."

Emily and Peggy plugged their phones into the wall sockets along the kitchen counter.

"But the big problem is," Emily continued. "When we're down at the lake, we're going to spend a half an hour or more on the Internet looking up the correct White House phone number. Once we find the number, who in the White House is going to believe us? How many times do you think we will be transferred before someone believes we're not crackpots? And then let's say, someone finally does believe us. How long will it take them to get the military mobilized and get here? There are two planes sitting out on that runway right now. By the time help arrives, the Vice President could already be flown to another location."

"She has a point, Peggy," Janice said. "I'm not saying I agree with her, but we need to come up with a better plan. Maybe we should go get him out of that shed. Once we get him, I'm sure he will know the correct phone number to call for help.

Peggy rolled her eyes at the two of them. "Okay," she said slowly. "You saw the men lock the shed with a padlock. How do you propose we get the door open when we go get him? I don't see any bolt cutters lying around here. And even if we did have them, the minute we snapped the lock on the door, the other men in the cabin would hear the cracking sound and be out of the cabin in a shot."

Emily put her jacket on and started for the door. "All these cabins are the same, right?" She looked back for confirmation. "So let's go look at this shed out back to see how it's built. Maybe we can figure something out." She turned around and said, "Come on. We don't have time to dilly-dally."

Peggy grabbed the keys to the shed right before she followed Janice and Emily out the door. "This is the dumbest thing we have ever gotten ourselves into," Peggy mumbled as she hustled along after her friends. She unlocked the door and they entered the shed.

When Emily stepped inside she pointed to the sidewall. "Aha! Just as I thought, these sheds have a window." She walked over to the wall and slid some boxes underneath the window. She climbed up to get a better look. The window was high up near the roof. It was also long and somewhat narrow, but it looked like a grown man could climb through it. It had a latch on the bottom. She turned the lock and pulled the window open, but she had to hold on to it, since it needed some sort of brace like a piece of wood to stay open. She looked down at the two women. There was a smile on her face. "We can do this. This is how we're going to get into the shed and rescue the Vice President."

Ever the skeptic, Peggy said, "You'll notice the lock is on the inside of the window and we're going to be standing outside. Just how do you propose getting the inside lock open, Wonder Women?"

"We'll break the glass and then reach in and unlock the window," Janice said. "We'll put one of our jackets over the window when we break it to muffle the sound."

Peggy looked down with her eyes tightly shut and held her head in her hands. "Oh, brother. I can't believe this is happening." She had a very worried look on her face when she looked up at her friends. "This scares me," she whispered.

"Me too," Janice answered with a slight nod of agreement. "But what else can we do? You saw the thug hit the Vice President in the face and the blood on the other man's face. I don't think we have a choice. Do you?"

Emily locked the window and climbed down from the boxes. "I want to look at the window from the outside of the shed." Once outside she stood under the side window and examined it. Her nose came up to the bottom of the window. "This is going to cause a problem. I think we're going to have to bring something to stand on in order to get the window opened. We're going to have to take a kitchen chair with us, because I don't think we'll be able to reach the window to climb into the shed. Then one of us will have stand on the chair in order to hold the window open. Let's go in and talk about this." She spoke calmly and seriously, because what they were about to do was dangerous. It had to be discussed and planned very carefully.

All were quiet on the way back to the cabin. Even when they were back inside, little was said. None of them felt courageous enough to even begin the discussion of rescuing the Vice President of the United States. Peggy suggested they have a light supper before they discussed what to do. The other two agreed, however, the three of them merely went through the motions of putting food on the table. When they sat down to eat, none of them felt hungry. Most of the food remained untouched.

As it began to get dark in the cabin for the sun had started to slide behind the mountains, Peggy got up and turned on the lights.

"Turn the lights off," Emily hissed. "Those men could be walking around out there right now, and for sure they'll see the lights coming from our windows."

Peggy immediately flipped the light switch to off. "Well, now what do we do? Pretty soon we won't be able to see our hands in front of our faces. We can't sit here in the dark."

"I've got it," Emily said. "The windows are only on the front of the cabin. Let's cover them with sheets and then use the flashlights on our phones for light. Peggy, do you have extra sheets somewhere?"

Peggy went to the cabinet and brought back sheets and pillowcases. Together the women hung sheets over the curtain rods of the windows and pillowcases over the door and the small window over the kitchen sink. She unplugged her cell phone and turned on the flashlight before laying it on the table face up. The small light of the phone allowed them to see in the cabin, but wasn't strong enough to create light through the sheets. "My batteries are going to be used up with the flashlight on, so we should plan on switching phones. That way at least one phone will be charging up at all times."

Janice got up and retrieved a pad of paper and pen from her purse. "We've got to talk about this. I'll take notes." She looked at the two women at the table. She slowly shook her head back and forth. There was such a sad look on her face. "I agree, Emily, we've got to help those people," she added quietly.

"I still think we should call for help," Peggy said. "We're just three old ladies up against all those men. What do you want to bet they have guns? We're not trained for this. We're not Navy Seals who know exactly what to do." She had her arms on the table and opened her hands in a helpless gesture. "Why don't we call the Sheriff's Department? They could help."

"Same thing as calling the White House," Emily said. "Who would believe us? And even if they did, they would probably send only one deputy up here to investigate. What if the men shot and killed him or her? I would never forgive myself for putting that person in harm's way."

Peggy snorted. "Yeah, but you have no compunction about our getting shot."

Emily winced at her friend's remark. "I understand how you feel," she said. "But didn't you see how frightened the Vice President was when we met him on the path? And now he and the other man are being kept in a shed. It's dark and it's cold. They've got to be frightened and terrified. Think about this. Like you said, once we free the Vice President, he'll know exactly which phone number to call at the White House. And I bet there's a code of some sort that he uses in order to alert them to the fact he's in trouble. I'm quite sure there's a specific procedure already in place for responding when he gives the code."

The emotions were over. Everyone spoke calmly as they discussed the pros and cons of calling for help versus trying to rescue the people. It was finally decided the three of them had to get the Vice President out of the shed themselves. Calling for help would come later.

"When do we do it?" Janice asked. "It's getting dark now. Should we go over after supper?"

"No," Emily answered. "The men in the cabin will still be awake. They may come out to check on things one last time before retiring for the night. If we go now it could end up they will have five hostages instead of two. So we need to go there sometime after 2:00 a.m. By then those men should all be asleep, and that will give us about four hours to do whatever else we need to do." Peggy and Janice had a look of confusion on their faces as they tried to process Emily's last remark.

"What?" she asked staring back at them. "Oh, I got it. What I meant by the four hours is, I'm counting on the fact that once those guys are asleep, no one will check on the Vice President until the morning. I'm guessing six o'clock at the earliest. By then we'll have the Vice President, and he should have made his phone call to the White House. And help will be on the way." The two nodded their heads in understanding.

Scared out of their wits realizing what they were about to do, the women started to discuss the best way to rescue the Vice President. It was decided they would start out at two o'clock in the morning. None of them were happy about having to carry a chair along with them, but they could see no other alternative to getting into the shed via the outside window. They would use their cell phones as flashlights. They debated about whether they would be able to break the window with the flashlight Emily found in a drawer or whether they would need a rock to do it. Janice solved the problem. She put on her coat and went outside. When she came back in she was carrying a large rock she had taken from the garden border around the front porch.

She showed them what she found and passed it around for them to hold and check out. "This should do the trick," she said.

"Once we break the window, who's going to go into the shed to help the men out?" Peggy asked. She looked at the other two. Neither could come up with an answer. "Okay, we do rock, paper, scissors. Loser goes into the shed. On three." The women shook their fists – one, two and three.

"Oh great, one rock, one paper, one scissors. Nobody loses. Let's do it again," Peggy said raising her fist.

"No wait. Stop," Emily said. "I'm going in the shed. I'm the one who talked you both into doing this. I'll be the one in the shed. It's settled. No arguments," she said when the other two were about to protest. "You two will stay outside and help us all get out of the shed. If something goes wrong and I'm caught, you make a run for it."

Janice wrote down the final plan and read it back to them. "Well, that's it then until two." She put her pencil and pad on the table. "Now what? Should we try to get a few hours of sleep? How about a good stiff drink? Lord knows I could use one. I cannot believe we're sitting here planning this. It's like we're in a bad dream."

Emily got up, went to the cupboard and took out three small glasses. She opened the refrigerator and took out a bottle of chilled Drambuie. After she poured the liquor into the glasses, she brought them to the table and passed them out. "Not exactly the drink of tough guys, is it? And I'm sure James Bond never threw back a Drambuie before he went on a mission, but this is all we've got." They raised their glasses. No one offered a toast. In fact, no one said a word as they downed their drinks.

Janice set her glass on the table and looked around. "I think it might be a good idea to turn the lights off in here. Those idiots may be walking around to check if anyone else is staying in these cabins. No use calling attention to ourselves before we even get started."

"It's not going to be easy sitting in the dark for the next six hours," Peggy said. "Maybe we should try to get some sleep. I'll set my phone alarm for quarter to two." She pulled her phone charger out of the wall socket and programmed the alarm. Emily made one error. She didn't recharge her phone. She left it sitting on the table.

It was agreed. The women cleared the table and washed the dinner dishes as best they could in the dark. They did all the preparations for going to bed – teeth brushed, faces washed and last bathroom call. But no one put on pajamas. They all lay on their beds with their clothes on. The day's hiking took its toll. And after much tossing and turning, they finally fell into an uneasy sleep.

• • •

Earlier that evening Amy's cell phone ID indicated the incoming call was from Nancy. "Hi. What's up, Nancy?"

"Have you heard anything from your mother yet?" Nancy asked.

"No. I told you I never hear from my mom until she gets back from a vacation. In fact, I bet you hear from your mother before I hear from mine. By the way, I thought you were going to try to get yourself calmed down."

"I've been working on it, but I can't change everything overnight. Thanks to your counseling, Professor, I'm getting my work and home life under control. I will say I scared the bejeebies out of my team when I told them we would meet only once a week," Nancy chuckled. "But worrying about my crazy mother is my last hurtle."

"Okay, last hurtle. You've got to work on not worrying about your mother," Amy said.

"I know, but the idea that she's out there in the wild and out of cell phone reach just bugs me. Only she would do something like this."

"Nancy, I'm sure the three of them are just fine. Knowing them, just like little Brownies, they're probably sitting around a campfire as we speak, roasting marshmallows, making S'mores. Stop worrying about your mom. She'll be just fine, and enjoy the rest of the evening with your family."

"You're right. After all, how much trouble can they get into when all you can do there is go hiking or canoeing? I'll calm down. I guess I just needed one of your pep talks."

CHAPTER 12

• • •

Peggy's cell phone alarm began to vibrate at one forty-five that morning. "Emily? Are you awake?" she whispered.

"Yeah. I've been awake for a while," Emily replied.

Janice turned in her bed. "Is it two o'clock?" she asked softly. "I don't know if I fell asleep or not. My eyes were closed, but it seems like I've been awake the whole time. Good grief. It's really dark in here. I can't even see my hand in front of my face. That doesn't bode well does it?"

Peggy reluctantly threw back the covers and got out of bed. "Let's get this over with. I hope to God it works." She looked in the general direction of the other bunks when she spoke. Because of the blackness in the cabin, she realized Janice was correct. She wasn't able to see a thing. "I'm sure we'll be able to see better once we're outside. Hopefully, the moon light will help guide us," Peggy said. "The moon is out, isn't it?"

The women fumbled around trying to find their jackets. Finally, Peggy turned on her cell phone flashlight and held it up. "I'm quite sure no one is skulking around outside at this time of night. I'm going to keep this on as we get ready and gather up everything we need."

"We're getting paranoid," Emily mumbled.

Once all jackets, hats and mittens were on, Emily made one last check to be sure they had everything. "I'm going to take my Swiss Army knife." She put it in the pocket of her jacket. "I don't know if the people will have been tied up or not. I hope we don't have to cut anything thicker than a clothesline rope. We don't have time to waste once I get in there. Janice do you have the rock for breaking the window?"

"Got it," Janice answered. "Do you think one of our parkas will be enough to muffle the sound of breaking glass? Maybe we should take one of the throw pillows from the sofa."

"No," Peggy said. "It's too thick. It would just absorb the force of the rock and not break the glass at all. We're going to go with a parka and hope to heaven it works." She took a chair from the kitchen table and carried it to the door.

Emily remained next to the table with her hands on the back of a chair. "Now listen. We have planned this as well as we can. We've tried to think of all the angles to get those men out of the shed." *Given the fact we don't know what the hell we're doing.* "So this is not the time to get squeamish. We have to stay as focused as we can, beginning right now."

Janice inhaled and let out a large breath of air. "Thanks. I think we all needed that pep talk, Emily." She walked over to the table and reached out for Emily's hand. "Come here, Peggy. Okay, everyone put your right hand out over the table. Just like sports teams do." When the three hands were one on top of the other, she said, "On three – we can do this. One, two, three."

"We can do this," the women whispered positively but quietly. With that they left the cabin.

Clouds were floating in the night sky and occasionally one blocked the moonlight. But when the moon was able to peek out from behind the clouds again, it provided enough light for the women to see the path to their destination. However, several times when the clouds completely covered the moon, they had to stop and then slowly inch their way along. Without the moonlight and not wanting to turn on their flashlights, it was total darkness in the woods. They could hear animals scurrying around them. Thankfully, it sounded like small animals. Even Emily and Peggy, the two wilderness mavens, were uneasy. They had never roamed the forest this late at night before. The women were forced to hold their arms out in front of them to avoid running into trees or bushes. The total darkness made their progress even slower. It took them almost twenty minutes to reach the side of the shed where the Vice President was being held captive.

From the moment the women left the cabin, they only spoke in whispers. Now that they were so near the last cabin where the men were sleeping, they put their heads directly next to the head of the person they were speaking to and whispered in their ear. They approached the shed cautiously.

CHAPTER 13

• • •

PEGGY SET THE KITCHEN CHAIR underneath the shed window. One thing was in their favor. Because of the slope of the land at this cabin, the ground under the window of the shed sat higher than the ground under the window of Peggy's shed. Therefore, even without the chair, the bottom of the window came up to the middle of the women's chests.

When Emily stood on the chair, she discovered her head was above the roof, and she had less than a three-foot climb to get her legs and feet through the window. She turned her cell phone flashlight on and peered into the shed. The two men inside had their hands and feet bound with duct tape. There was tape covering the Vice President's mouth. He had a frantic look in his eyes as he saw the light shining through the window, so she shined the light on her face and put her finger to her lips indicating he remain quiet. *Oh boy. With this light directly under my face, my double chins are being highlighted. With this ghoulish face staring at him if he was scared before, the*

Vice President must really be terrified now. Emily gave herself an internal thunk on the head. *This is no time for stand-up comedy, you idiot.*

Emily removed her parka and held it over the window. She motioned to Janice to bring the stone and get up on the chair with her. She made a hitting movement to indicate breaking the window. Janice nodded in understanding and joined Emily on the chair.

"Hit the window about six inches above the lock," she whispered into Janice's ear. "That way I can get my hand in to unlock it without having to break the glass more than once."

Janice hesitated not knowing if the parka would be enough to muffle the sound of breaking glass. She looked over at Emily with a worried look on her face. Finally, she swallowed. Her face had a grimace as she brought the rock back and hit the window right where Emily told her. The rock created a jagged hole in the window and the sound was barely audible. The women breathed sighs of relief. Emily let her jacket fall to the ground before reaching in to unlatch the lock. Janice raised it up and held it so Emily could crawl through.

Before going in, Emily put her head through the window and shined her flashlight down to see if there were any crates stacked underneath. There were. She turned to Janice, mouthed the word "crates" and gave her a thumbs up.

She put her cell phone in her pants pocket. Then she swung one leg over the window ledge, bent her body forward and went in sideways. She hung on to the side of the frame while she pulled her body through. It was pitch black inside. She slowly lowered herself and was able to put one leg on the crate. Still holding onto the window frame, she turned toward the wall and pulled her other leg into the shed and stood on the crate. Before getting down she reached into her pants pocket, pulled out her phone and turned the light on. Once she got off the crates, she laid it on the floor to free up her hands so she could cut the men free of the duct tape. By now her antics caused the other man to roll over to watch her. He moaned as he turned toward her.

When she tried to reach into the pocket of her parka to retrieve the Swiss Army knife, she realized she wasn't wearing the parka. It was used to break the window and she had dropped it on the ground before climbing in. The knife was in the jacket pocket that was now outside. She hurried over to the crates and climbed up. "My jacket," she hissed to Janice. "The knife is in the pocket."

Janice looked at Peggy standing next to the chair and motioned she needed the jacket lying on the ground. Peggy understood, rushed over picked it up and handed it to Janice who held it up to the window. While Janice held it up, Emily reached through the window and searched the pockets. A look of relief spread across her face when her fingers wrapped around the knife. She ducked back into the shed and climbed down once again. She looked at the two captives. Their eyes showed pure terror. *After my up and down antics, I hope they understand we're here to rescue them.*

She made the decision that the best way to begin freeing them was going to be to cut the duct tape wrapped around their wrists. That would free them to work on getting the tape off their own mouths. She did not relish having to pull it off herself. And because their arms had been bound behind their backs, freeing the wrists first would allow the circulation to flow again before they would be required to climb out the window.

As she was walking over to the Vice President, she heard someone at the door. For a nanosecond, she froze. *The phone!!!* She took two steps to the side, swooped down and picked it up. Because she was now holding the knife in one hand and the phone in the other, she didn't have the time to find the icon to shut the light off! *I need to hide!* She could hear the lock being removed from the latch. Frantically, she looked at the opposite wall. There was a canoe upside down on sawhorses. She made a dive for it at the same time she shoved the lighted phone underneath her shirt with the face toward her belly. She scooted to the front of the canoe and scrunched herself up into a ball as best she could under the tip. She heard the door open. A person entered shining a flashlight. Now she could see there were a few pieces of equipment in front of tip of the canoe and that helped give her some cover. She looked down at her shirt to make sure there was no light coming from her phone. *Holy shit. What if my phone starts to ring with some stupid robo-call!!* She didn't dare try to shut it off now.

Outside the other two women were plastered with their backs against the side of the shed. Fortunately, Peggy had spotted the faint movement of light coming down the path from the cabin before the man had even gotten near the shed. She immediately alerted Janice who was able to quietly lower the window and step off the chair before the man reached the door. Just like her shed, if a person were walking toward the front of the shed, they wouldn't be able to see along the side of it. Nevertheless, they were terrified as they tried to conceal themselves.

CHAPTER 14

• • •

WHEN THE MAN ENTERED, HE shined his flashlight at the Vice President and walked to the middle of the shed. It was Jim Kovac, the Secret Service Agent who sold his soul for the thirty pieces of silver. He paid no attention to the other man lying next to him. "I have to make my check-in call to Washington," he said.

Oh, thank God. The Secret Service agent. One of the good guys. He'll know what to do, Emily thought.

"I thought you'd like to hear me relay the message that you're sleeping and everything is okay," Agent Kovac said with a sneer in his voice.

"I did this for the money, you know. Why should I be paid peanuts risking my life for some two-bit politician? " There was such derision in his voice bordering on hatred.

What the heck is going on? Emily could see him raise the phone to his ear. "Bob, this is Jim checking in. The Vice President is all tucked in and sleeping like a baby. All quiet here. Ten-four." He hung up the phone. "I won't be seeing you again, Bill. Enjoy your life. What little is left of it." His chuckle sounded evil as he turned to leave the shed.

Please, please, please. Don't see the broken glass on the floor.

Emily heard him shut and lock the door. Even though a huge wave of relief washed over her, she was unable to move out of the position under the canoe. She began to breath slowly in and out through her mouth. She listened until she thought she heard the door of the cabin close before she crawled out and took the lighted phone from beneath her shirt. She looked over at the two men. Trying to give them an encouraging smile that failed her. On wobbly legs, she walked over to the Vice President and started cutting the binding on his wrists. As she was cutting she whispered in his ear, "My friends and I are here to get you out. You have to remain as silent as you can. If you have to speak, do it in a whisper. We can't take the chance the men in the cabin won't hear us."

She moved over to the man who had been beaten and noticed there was no duct tape covering his mouth. He was moaning in pain, and he looked a mess. Blood was dripping out of his mouth. *Thank goodness the goons didn't put tape over his mouth. He would have choked to death.* She had to repeat her message of rescue and silence to him twice. *What have they done to you?* After she cut the tape around his wrists, she helped him move his arms around. She then freed his legs and those of the Vice President.

She went to the window, opened it and looked out. She saw her two friends still plastered to the side. They looked up at her. Janice mouthed, "Oh my God." Her eyes were like saucers.

"You okay?" Peggy whispered.

Emily shook her head in agreement. She motioned for Peggy to get on the chair. "It was the Secret Service agent. He's gone now, but it sounds like he's out for money. I'll explain later. I'm going to get these guys out of here. But the man who was beaten is going to need help." Peggy made an OK sign.

Emily ducked back inside and knew they had to get away from here as soon as possible. She did not want another scare like they had just experienced. By now the Vice President was standing and helping the other man. The only problem was, when he got him up, he seemed too weak and had to sit down again.

"You are going to go out the window," she whispered to the two of them. "There are two women out there who will help you climb out."

Both of the men had a look of skepticism on their face when they heard the news that their rescuers were women. Emily rolled her eyes and groaned. *In this day and age, what difference does it make who does the rescuing?* "Once outside, it's even more important not to make a sound. We are going to take you to our cabin. When we get there, you'll be free to talk. Okay?" She looked at each one of them as she said this.

"Mr. Vice President, I'm going to ask you to stay behind and help me get this gentleman through the window. He looks very hurt and getting him out won't be easy. Will you do that?"

"Absolutely," the Vice President answered.

They turned to the man. "Can you tell me where your injuries are, sir?" Emily whispered.

"Roken haw and teeh. Hink rib crack, kick mee in legh," he said as quietly as he could.

"You have a broken jaw and some of your teeth are knocked out?" The man nodded his head slightly. "Which side is your rib broken?" He pointed to his right side. "Which leg did they kick?" Again he pointed to the right. There was a mixture of sadness and anger on her face. She laid a hand on his arm hoping it was one place where he wasn't in pain. "I'm so sorry, sir."

She looked up at Vice President Andersen. "We're going to have to lift him through the window. I think we should . . . " She looked down at the man. "Where is your rib broken, front or back?" He moaned and just moved his hand around in a circle over the right side of his rib cage. She put her hand over her mouth and blew out a breath of air trying to figure out how best to get him out.

The Vice President stood with his hands on his hips. "Whatever we do, we have to be careful not to let any area of his rib cage touch the window frame as he goes out." Emily silently nodded her agreement.

She bent down and whispered in the man's ear. "Did you hear what Vice President Andersen said? We will be as careful as we can and try very hard not to let your rib cage touch the window frame. You can't make a sound, not one sound."

He winced when he tried to nod his head in agreement. "Waaan out," he said softly. Emily and Vice President Andersen smiled sadly at his determination.

"We're going to get you out," the Vice President said. As gently as they could, they helped him to his feet. He had trouble getting onto the crate under the window. Finally, the Vice President climbed up and held the man under his arms and pulled him up as quickly as he could while Emily pushed on the man's rear-end. Once up, she too climbed up and motioned for Peggy to come close.

"His ribs have been broken on the right side," she whispered. "So don't grabbed him in the chest area when you help him through." Peggy nodded her head indicating she understood.

"Good luck," the Vice President whispered. "We'll try to be as gentle as we can, sir." The man was able to raise his arms and hold on the to top of the window frame. The two of them steadied him and pushed him up, again by bracing his rear-end, so he could swing both legs through the window. As he arched his back while sliding out, he moaned softly, but not loud enough for the moan to carry very far.

Peggy helped to steady the man on the other side. Janice guided his legs to the chair. Once he was out completely, Peggy stepped off the chair while still keeping her hands on his waist to steady him. She and Janice motioned for the man to put his hands on their shoulders in order to get down from the chair.

Emily turned to the Vice President. "Okay, Mr. Vice President, you're next."

"No, I'll go after you," he said.

This night was one of the scariest nights in Emily's life. She and her friends had gotten involved in a sinister plot right out of a Hollywood movie. Something snapped. She ran out of patience with his stoicism. Without even thinking about to whom she was speaking, she hissed, "This isn't negotiable. Now get your ass through that window and quit wasting time. Damn it" She immediately dropped her head and whispered "Sorry" as she realized what she just said to the Vice President of the whole United States!

His head popped up and he jerked back at her words. But then with a smirk on his face, he said "Yes, Ma'am" and gave her a jaunty salute. He grabbed the top of the window frame, swung his legs through and slowly slid out. He was in good physical shape.

Before Emily left, she climbed down to retrieve her cell phone still sitting on the ground with the light still on. She gathered up a few spools of duct tape lying on the floor and put them on her wrists like bracelets. Just before she turned to leave, she spotted a coil of thin rope on one of the crates. For some reason it seemed important, so she put her arm through it and hoisted it onto her shoulder. After she climbed out, she lowered the window, reached in and locked it. She didn't want it to start banging if the wind happened to pick up during the rest of the night.

Janice and Peggy led the way back to their cabin. The two walked with the injured man between them. He had his arms linked through theirs to keep his balance. Figuring they had made it out safely and no one would be awake in the cabin, Emily turned on the flashlight to guide them back. They no longer had to creep along when the moon went behind a cloud.

The Vice President walked next to Emily. He had grabbed the chair and was carrying it. When she tried to protest, he had a slight smile on his face. "This isn't negotiable. Now get your ass down that path and quit wasting time," he whispered in her ear. She grinned and gave him a salute just like he did.

CHAPTER 15

• • •

WHEN THEY CAME UP TO the next cabin, Peggy turned on the light of her cell phone and kept it on while they made their escape. With both lights to guide them, they made it back to their cabin in less than 10 minutes.

They decided not turn on any lights inside the cabin. Peggy laid her cell phone on the kitchen table with the flashlight on. They helped the injured man sit at the table. They were finally able to take a close look at him. One eye was swollen shut and blood was dripping out of his mouth. He looked like he was in a great deal of pain.

"Okay, here's the deal," Emily announced. She looked at the Vice President and the injured man. "You both need some time to calm down." "The bathroom is over there in the corner. There are towels and washcloths for you to use. When you're finished, come have some orange juice and a bite to eat. This has been an ordeal for you. Janice and I will take care of this gentleman," she said. "By the way, who the hell are you?" she asked looking down at the man.

"Eye-let," he said. The women stared at him in confusion.

"He's the pilot of the twin engine plane that brought Weber's two men here," the Vice President responded. "When he learned I was being kidnapped, he started to balk. That's when they beat him."

"Do you know his name?" Janice asked the Vice President.

He shook his head. "No," he said on his way to the bathroom to wash up.

"Car...ral," he man said.

Janice gently put an arm around his shoulder. "Did you say Carl?"

After the stress on his jaw with each step he took on the way back to the cabin, Carl could no longer move his head without being in extreme pain. He merely rocked back and forth and said, "Yah, Car...ral."

Emily emptied a tray of ice cubes in a bowl and added water. She was soaking several dishcloths in the cold mixture. "Okay Carl, we've got to start fixing you up and making you more comfortable." She wrung out two cold cloths and told him to hold one on his swollen eye. She knew she had to stop the bleeding of his broken teeth, but she didn't know if he could open his mouth. She held the second cloth out to him. "Can you open your mouth and hold this cloth against your front teeth?" He took it and winced as he put a corner of it into the gap of his missing upper-front teeth.

In the meantime, Janice rummaged around in her backpack. "Carl needs some pain medicine. I packed something with Ibuprofen in it. Ah, here it is," she said holding up the bottle. "Carl, do you think you could swallow some pills?"

"Nah. Can't oo-pen mout," he said pointing to his jaw.

Janice looked at him for a moment. "Um, could you swallow a spoonful of water?"

He began rocking back and forth. "Yah."

She went to the counter and took a large knife from the drawer. Using the hilt she began crushing two pills. After she put the powder in a tablespoon, she added a little orange juice and went back to the table. "Okay, love. This is going to taste awful, but it should give you some relief."

Carl took the cloth compress out of his mouth and put his hand on Janice's hand to guide it as she brought the spoon to his lips. Slowly he managed to swallow the entire tablespoon of the mixture. He grimaced. "Ugh," he said. Janice brought the orange juice back to the table and filled the spoon again. He managed to get two more spoonfuls down to wash away the taste.

"I think we need to tie a scarf around his head to keep his jaw in place," Peggy said. She went over to the coat rack and brought her multi-colored scarf back. She looped it under his chin and gently tied the ends on top of his head. The two ends of the scarf drooped down each side of his head. The women smiled at her creation.

"Well, you're not going to be asked to pose for a men's fashion magazine, but you do look cute," Janice said and gave him a wink.

Emily was rummaging around in the cupboard drawers looking for a large dishtowel. "Now I want to put your right arm in a sling. I think it will help keep the stress off your rib cage. What do you say?" Carl rocked back and forth. When she found what she was looking for, she brought it to the table and folded it into a triangle. She gently worked on securing his arm in it and then tying the two ends together at the back of his neck.

"Carl, didn't you tell me those men kicked you in the leg?" she asked. "We better take a look at that too." Janice and Emily helped Carl stand up. After he made several failed attempts trying to unbuckle his belt, Janice got on her knees in front of him and unfastened the belt. As she was lowering the zipper of his fly, she started to chuckle. She looked up at him and said, "You know under different circumstances, in this position you and I look like we're involved in making a porn movie." That broke some of the tension. Everyone began to laugh. Carl held onto his jaw as he giggled.

"I heard that," the Vice President said with a smile on his face as he walked out of the bathroom wiping his face with a towel.

"Your daughter would faint if she heard you talking like that," Emily told Janice. She looked at the Vice President. "Before we go any farther with our Clare Barton slash "Debbie Does Dallas" nursing act, could you help him to the bathroom?" She looked back at Carl and grinned. "Or would you rather have Janice help you?"

"Naaaah," Carl responded as he hiked up his pants and held on tightly while he walked toward the bathroom with the Vice President.

When the two men came out and back to the table, the Vice President said, "Maybe we can put a cold compress on Carl's leg while we're eating. He can keep his pants on with the compress." He gave Janice a wink.

Peggy prepared toast for everyone and poured glasses of orange juice. "Please eat," she said. "And then we've got to talk."

Vice President Andersen said, "I need to call the White House. But they took my phone away from me."

"Don't worry, Mr. Vice President, Emily said. "We've got that covered. Because there's no phone connection in the cabin, one of us will take you down to the lake so you can make your call using one of our phones. But first you eat something. It will help release some of the horrible tension of what you've been through."

"Everyone," Emily announced. "Take a deep breath. We did it!" Her face lit up with a big smile as she raised her glass of orange juice. Everyone including the Vice President had tears in their eyes as the reality of what they had been through and what they had accomplished hit home.

The Vice President took only a few bites of toast before he looked over at the women. "Look, I've really got to make the phone call and let the people at the White House know what's going on. Once I make it, help should be on the way. Then we'll be safe."

Emily put her piece of toast back on her plate. "You're right," she said as she stood up and retrieved her coat and hat. She took her phone off the kitchen table and shut down the flashlight app. Peggy turned her phone back on with the flashlight and set it on the table.

Emily looked at the Vice President. "Ready? Let's go. It will only take a few minutes to reach the lake."

Peggy got two sets of bells from the counter and handed them to Emily and the Vice President. "You better put these on. I think we pushed our luck as far as we could tonight. And I doubt you'll be heard because it's only a little before 4 a.m."

"What are these for?" the Vice President asked when Peggy handed him the set of the bells.

"You attach them to the bottom of your jacket. The sound helps to keep the bears and cougars away." She scrunched up her face, because she knew he wouldn't be happy to learn they didn't bring the bells when they went to rescue him. They could have met up with wild animals on the way here.

"Now you tell me?" he said in a raised voice.

Emily laid her hand on his arm. "Mr. Vice President, when we came to get you out of the shed, it was vital not to make a sound.

We had to chance it then. And it did work. We got you out and we didn't run into any large animals roaming around."

He dropped his head and stared at the floor for a moment. He raised his head. "I understand. I'm sorry. It's been a trying day."

Emily patted his arm and gave him a small smile. "Not a problem. Come on. Let's go."

CHAPTER 16

• • •

ON THE WAY DOWN TO the lake, Emily turned the phone flashlight back on. She figured they would be safe. It was still too early for the men in the other cabin to be up and checking on the shed. And besides, the bells were tinkling away, so what difference would a flashlight make? When they reached the shore of the lake, she gave her phone to the Vice President. "You should be able to make your call from here. It'll be nice to have this mess over with."

The Vice President began to dial a special phone number that was used only in emergencies. When he entered the last digit but before he pressed send, Emily's phone went dark. He turned it off and then on again, but it remained dark. "I think your phone just ran out of power," he said. The looked on his face bordered on panic.

"What!" Emily hissed. "Oh, my god. I forgot to recharge it during the night. I'm so sorry. Then I used it as a flashlight the whole time we were in the shed and again just now in the cabin. Dear lord. I'm so sorry, Mr. Vice President." She was frantic and grabbed his arm. "Come on let's get back to the cabin. Hopefully Peggy's phone is still charged up and we can use hers." She turned away and began to scramble up the path.

When they rounded the corner of the cabin, it was dark. *Oh, this doesn't bode well. Why can't we see light from Peggy's cell phone?* When they got inside the cabin, they had their answer. Peggy's phone was out of juice too, because she kept it on all night when she set her alarm.

"Not to panic," Janice said. She fumbled around in the dark and managed to turn on a small lamp sitting on an end table next to the couch. "Emily and Peggy should have their phones usable in an hour, Mr. Vice President. And you should have time to get back down to the lake safely before the men begin to stir in the other cabin." She tried to keep her voice positive and reassuring.

Peggy's hands trembled as she plugged in her phone. As terrified as she was about all the dead phones and being completely shut off from the outside world right now, she tried to assure herself that within an hour they would be able to call for help. She felt the most important thing to do now was to keep everyone calm and the panic level down. "I agree with Janice. We're going to be fine," she announced. "Recharging won't take that long. We have time. Everyone come and sit at the table. We haven't had time to talk and we can do it now." She pulled out a chair and sat down. One by one the others came to join her.

Emily looked around at the people sitting at the table. "What happened to Carl?" she asked.

Janice pointed to a lounge chair in the sitting area. "He's sleeping. That's the best thing for him right now."

Emily turned to the Vice President. "I think you should know how we knew you were in trouble and the plans we made to rescue you. Actually, it was Janice who knew you needed help. She spent the next several minutes explaining how they realized he was in trouble and snuck back to Webber's cabin and watched as he and Carl were locked in the shed. Then she told about the plans and decisions they made to help him.

Janice looked over at the Vice President. "Mr. Vice President, why on earth are you up here with that horrible Patrick Webber? And why has he done this to you?"

"Yeah, and what about that Secret Service man in the shed who deserted you?" Emily interjected.

"I've been asking myself those same questions," Bill Andersen replied. "Patrick Webber told the President he wanted to help mend some fences between the far-right members of Congress and the President, but he said we needed to get as far away from the Press as we could. He wanted to meet with me to discuss the issues and let us know how he would work with the other ultra-conservatives. That's why we flew here to Montana. He felt it was time for everyone to work together."

Emily and Nancy snorted when they heard that one. "Yeah, right," Emily retorted

"I know. I know," he said with an embarrassed look on his face. He continued with his head down. His voice sounded tired. He rubbed his forehead as he spoke. "Anyway, the President and I discussed it and given the enormous chasm in our country today, we felt it was worth listening to what he had to say. However, when we landed his two goons were waiting for us. They overpowered one of my Secret Service Agents and put him back on the jet. I just hope he's still alive." He had to stop for a moment before continuing as he thought about his Agent. "Apparently, Webber bought off my other Agent. As we walked to the cabin, he told me his real plan. I was going to be flown into the wilds of Canada and killed. He would then talk the President into choosing a Vice President he wanted – one of his cronies, in short, an ultra-conservative whom he could then control. Once that was done, after a while he planned to have the President assassinated, so then by the laws of our Constitution his man would become President and the Conservatives would finally be in power. Or as Patrick put it, *he* would be in power." The Vice President had such a sad on his face. He silently shook his head back and forth. By now Emily and Janice sat there with their hands over their mouths as they were trying to digest what he was saying.

Janice looked at the people around the table. "Dear God," she whispered. "This can't be happening."

"It gets better," he said. "After I was killed, Webber was going to make it look like I was killed by Middle-East terrorists."

"I can't even wrap my arms around something as diabolical as this," Emily said.

The Vice President shrugged his shoulders. "Think of our history. Plots like this to assassinate the president are not uncommon. I don't think we'll ever know the truth about who was really behind the assassinations of President Kennedy and President Lincoln. President McKinley was also assassinated. The history books tell us he was shot by a deranged man. Maybe there was a conspiracy in that one too. And look at all the pot shots other Presidents endured." He held up his hand to count on his fingers. Starting with his index finger, he said, "President Teddy Roosevelt was shot in Milwaukee, Wisconsin." He continued to count on his fingers. "There was the man who broke into the White House with plans to shoot President Truman, the woman who tried to kill President Ford, and the young man who shot President Reagan." He gave a slight snort and had a sad smile on his face. "This is the second time in our history that a Vice President has been targeted."

Peggy had a frown on her face. "Second time? Who was the other Vice President?"

"Andrew Johnson. He was Lincoln's Vice President and the plot was to assassinate both of them and send the North into disarray. But the plot to kill Johnson never took place."

"Huh. I never knew that."

Bill looked across the table at the three old ladies and smiled as he shook his head. "I want to thank the three of you for what you did for me. Last night in the shed, I was sure I would be killed."

Emily got flustered at his words. The Vice President of the United States was thanking them. In her embarrassment, she waved her hand in a dismissive gesture. "No thanks are necessary."

"Too bad we aren't part of the British Empire anymore. You could knight us and make us "Dames". Peggy had a twinkle in her eye.

"Yeah and never underestimate Senior Citizens either." Janice nodded her head for emphasis.

Bill Andersen smiled at them. "I won't."

Peggy saw him look over at the two phones sitting on counter. She looked at her watch. It was now 5:10 a.m. "Listen, Mr. Vice President. Give those phones about an hour to be sure they get fully charged. At 6 o'clock you can go down to the lake and make your call."

Emily nodded her head in complete agreement. "Just as a precaution, why don't we turn the lamp off now and take the sheets off the windows?"

"It's still going to be quite dark in here, Emily." Janice said.

"I don't think anyone over there is awake yet and checking the shed, but we need to make this cabin look deserted, and we might as well do it now. By the way, Mr. Vice President, do you think we could call you Bill? Considering the circumstances we're all in, Mr. Vice President seems a mite too formal right now."

Bill nodded his head in agreement. "I have no problem whatsoever with that, Emily."

The four of them took the sheets off the windows and threw them on one of the beds next to the back wall. Even though the living room area windows had lace curtains only on the bottom half, it was still very dark when Janice turned the table lamp off. "It's getting very cold in here. Maybe we should put our jackets on to keep warm," she said.

CHAPTER 17

• • •

THE VICE PRESIDENT WAS SITTING with Janice and Emily on the couch in the living area conversing in whispers so they wouldn't disturb Carl. Now that the windows were uncovered, it made them feel more exposed, like they were in a fish bowl. Waiting for the phones to charge seemed like an eternity.

Earlier Peggy had covered Carl with a blanket. She listened to his deep breathing. *Good. The longer and the deeper you sleep, the more healing you'll be doing.* She got up and walked to the counter to check the time on her phone. It was still too dark to see her wrist watch. It was 5:40 a.m. She checked both phones. Even though neither of them indicated the charge was complete, she felt there was enough juice in them to get down to the lake for the call to the White House. "I think you can go down to the lake to make your call now, Bill." But then she froze. She could hear leaves crunching outside. Someone was coming up the path to the cabin. She whirled around in the direction of the couch. "Get down!" she hissed in a frantic whisper.

The others must have heard the crunching too, because the three of the scrambled off the couch then crawled and ducked down underneath the front windows. Peggy remembered there was a frying pan still sitting on the drain board from last night's dinner. She groped for the handle in the dark and picked it up and stood against the wall next to the door. She held the pan high with two hands as if she were going to swing a baseball bat. By now the person was on the porch of the cabin and rattling the door handle. *It has to be one of the men from the other cabin. Why are they up so early?* The man walked over to the front windows and peered in using a flashlight. Fortunately, Carl was in the chair facing away from the window. They were safe, Peggy thought.

"Oh, no. Our backpacks!" Emily said in a frantic whisper when she turned around and followed the beam of light to the far wall. She could see the three backpacks next to the unmade beds with the heap of sheets that had covered the windows. She whipped her head toward Janice, "Oh God. What do we do now?"

Janice opened her mouth but didn't even have time to reply, because the man immediately returned to the door and smashed the window. His hand reached in to unlock the door. The door flew open. Peggy was barely able to jump out of the way before it hit the wall where she was standing. She was still in her baseball stance with the frying pan held high. When the man entered, he looked to the left. By the size of him Peggy could tell it was one of the beefcakes. Without waiting one second more, Peggy swung the pan with all her strength and hit him along side of his head. He dropped like a boulder to the floor. Everyone felt the vibration. A gun fell out of his hand. Peggy stood motionless in shock at what she had just done.

The crash woke Carl. He moaned as he tried to turn in the chair. Bill, Janice and Emily shot up and came over. Janice had to pry the pan from Peggy's fingers as she stood there staring down. Emily the planner groped around the counter trying to locate the duck tape she had taken from the other shed.

The Vice President squatted down and felt for a pulse on the man's neck. "He's alive but still unconscious," he said to no one in particular.

"Here," Emily said holding out a roll of tape. "We have to hurry and tape him up. He's way too big for us to subdue if he comes to." She rolled him over and began wrapping tape around his wrists. "Obviously, they now know your gone, Bill."

"Looks' like it. I'm so sorry the three of you have been caught up in this."

"Forget the . . . 'I'm sorry bit'," Peggy said coming out of her stupor. She bent down and by feel located the gun the man had dropped. She picked up it up and put it in her jacket pocket. "What the hell are we going to do now? We can't leave him lying here in the middle of the floor, and the broken window will be a dead giveaway to the others that something happened in this cabin."

Emily finished taping the man's feet. "Well, it seems to me we have to go to Plan B. We get rid of him. Get down to the lake for a phone call so the troops are on the way. And then . . .and then we try to get ourselves to a safe place and wait."

"While the other two men with guns run around and try to kill us!" Janice looked over at Emily. She looked down at the huge man on the floor. "You think the four of us can drag this guy to your shed, Peggy? It's still dark out. Hopefully, each of the other men went in different directions and none of them will see us dragging him there."

"Well, whatever we do, we have to do it fast," Bill said. The women nodded their heads in agreement.

"And we now have a gun," Peggy said taking the man's gun out of her pocket. "At least we have some chance against the others."

"Do you know anything about how to shoot a gun?" Bill asked Peggy.

"No."

He held out his hand. "Give it to me then. Look, maybe we should just leave him here and get ourselves down to the lake." Then he stopped and pursed his lips together lost in thought. "Patrick Webber is going to get away, you know. And my Secret

Service Agent is being held prisoner in Webber's jet. If Webber gets there, I'm almost certain, he'll kill Agent Daniels before he leaves . . . probably just toss him out and leave him on the ground. I can't let that happen. I have to try to rescue him." It was too dark to see his face clearly, but the ladies could hear the anger and desperation in his voice.

"Okay. Here's the deal," Peggy said. "First we get this man into the shed. Being in there will make it hard for the others to find him, and it will keep the nut jobs with guns out there down to just two. I'm assuming Webber is too much of a weenie to join in the search. You're right, Bill. Now that he knows you've escaped, he's probably trying to get out of here and has no intention of bringing his men along with him. What a creep."

Emily, ever the planner, assessed the situation regarding Webber and the Secret Service Agent. "Okay, let's make it fast while it's still dark and this behemoth is still unconscious. The four of us should be able to drag him to the shed. Two of us will pull him under his arms and two of us will sort of pull him by his belt. Once we're done with that then we can firm up plans to get your Agent to safety. Get the key for the lock on the shed door, Peggy. I've got the duct tape. Wait a minute. I want to bring the rope I took from the other shed. Don't know if we'll need it, but can't hurt to bring it with us."

Luckily, Peggy had little trouble feeling and locating the shed key in the drawer. The rope was on the counter right where Emily had left it. By this time, Carl had risen and was sitting up. "Waan to help," he said. He started to get out of the chair.

"No" they said in unison. "You stay here. We can manage," Peggy told him.

Bill took his arm and sat him back in the chair. "You need to take care of yourself. We can do this ourselves. We'll be back as soon as we get him settled in the shed." Carl didn't offer much of an argument as he leaned back in the chair.

When the four of them tried to drag the man to the door, it proved more difficult than they thought. He was so big and must have weighed well over 250 pounds. Before Emily opened it, she said, "Now when we're outside, not one word. Ready?" The three whispered, "Yes." Out the door they went.

When they had the man inside Peggy's shed, they laid him on his side. He groaned and made a feeble attempt to move his arms and legs. He still seemed groggy and offered little resistance when they tried to subdue him.

No one brought a phone for light, but the moon was now out in full and they were able to see somewhat inside the shed. "What if he moves around and starts kicking on the walls of the shed to draw attention?" Janice asked.

Emily took the rope she brought and slung one end around the canoe. "I'm going to tie this end around his chest. If he tries to move, the canoe will fall on him. You guys check his pockets for a cell phone, and make sure it's turned off. We don't need any ringing while we're trying to keep out of sight."

That rope around the canoe seems awfully cruel," Janice whispered.

"What's cruel, Janice? This was one of the men who beat the daylights out of Carl, and he had a gun when he came to get us. If it wasn't for Peggy, I'm sure he would have killed us." Emily went down on one knee and tapped the man on the face. "Hey. Can you hear me?"

By now the man was lucid. There was pure fury in his eyes. Because of the tape on his mouth he could only make muffled sounds. He started to thrash around and kick his legs. The strain on the rope pulled on the canoe. Fortunately, Bill was able to grab it before it fell, "Hey, knock it off," Emily said in the man's face. "Do you see this rope? It's tied around that canoe. You keep thrashing like that and you're going to pull it down right on top of you, so just stop it." Even though he couldn't speak, Emily felt he would murder her if he got the chance. It was quite unnerving. "Listen. We're going to contact the White House and pretty soon this place will be swarming with soldiers. We'll let them know you're in the shed. You should be out of here by this afternoon. Which is more than you would have done for us." Her lip curled in a sneer as she looked at him. She stood up. "Let's get out of here," she said as she herded the rest of them through the door.

CHAPTER 18

• • •

ONCE THEY WERE BACK IN the cabin, they gathered around Carl in the living area to discuss the next steps they had to take. Bill stood up and began pacing back and forth in front of the fireplace. He seemed lost in thought. The four of them watched him and were wise enough to give him the time to do some thinking. He stopped and faced them. "Okay. Here's what we're going to do. I'm going down to get my Agent out of the plane before Webber does anything to him. The call to the White House will just have to wait. Agent Daniels is my first concern right now, and I'm hoping he still has his phone. If he does I can make a call right there. As a precaution I'll take one of your phones with me. You four are going to stay here. You've all been through more than enough. I can't involve you any further in this mess."

"No way are you going to do this alone."

"Think again if you think we're just going to sit here."

"Waan help."

"The discussion is over, Bill. We're in this with you."

Bill stared down at the four of them while slowly shaking his head. His lips were clamped together but he had a slight smile, one eyebrow was raised. "You know Senior Citizens are really a pain in the shorts." He took in a deep breath of air and let it out. "Okay, here's the deal. We can't all go get my Agent. I'll take one of you with me and the other two stay here with Carl. He needs more time to heal. In fact, why don't you give him another dose of pain medicine?"

"I'll go with you," Janice said.

"No, I think I should go," Emily answered.

Janice stood and walked to the kitchen area. She took two spools of duct tape off the counter. "No, Emily. You were the one who went into the shed. Now it's my turn, and Peggy needs to stay here to help defend the realm with the frying pan." She turned and gave Peggy a slight smile as she came back in the living area. She set the tape on the table and retrieved her jacket. While she was stuffing the tape in her pockets, she looked at Emily. "Where is your knife? I think we'll need that."

Emily retrieved it from her jacket and handed it to Janice. "I can still be the one to go."

Janice put Emily's knife in her pocket and didn't even answer her friend. She turned to Bill. "Ready to go?"

He zipped up his jacket. "Are you sure you want to do this, Janice?"

Her shoulders slumped. She dropped her chin then raised her eyes as if she were looking over the top of reading glasses and glared at him without saying a word. He held up his hands in surrender. "Okay, okay. You're coming with me."

"Have you got the gun?" she asked.

He nodded and patted his jacket pocket. "Yup, right here." He looked at the three remaining people and hesitated. He didn't want to leave them here while men were still out there with guns, but he didn't think he had any other choice. Five people, one of them barely able to walk, would only slow him down. Certainly Emily and Peggy proved they were more than capable of taking care of each other and Carl. "We'll be back as soon as we can. I think you'll be safe inside the cabin."

"Go, go," Peggy said shooing them to the door. She tried to sound positive and in control, but deep down she was terrified. If the other men discovered them here, would it be like shooting fish in a barrel?

Emily came to stand beside her and put her arm around Peggy's shoulder. "Yeah, the sooner you get going the faster we're going to get out of this mess." After Bill and Janice left, Emily looked over at Peggy and saw tears were running down her cheeks.

"Oooh, boy," Emily whispered. She tightened her arm around Peggy's shoulder and gave her a slight shake. "Come on we've got things to do. You give Carl some orange juice and pain medicine. I'm going to clear up the beds and stash our backpacks in the bathroom. If anyone else does come peeking in the windows again, this cabin has to look *un-ocupado*. But ah . . . keep that frying pan within reach."

CHAPTER 19

• • •

BILL AND JANICE WALKED DOWN to the path in front of the cabin. He raised his chin to indicate they needed to turn to the left. "I remember we came up on a path between the next two cabins when we walked here from the airstrip." He kept his voice low. Janice just nodded as she walked beside him.

She watched him take the gun out of his pocket. He kept it at his side. She felt some comfort in that. Still, being out in the open with men running around with guns ready to shoot them was unnerving. She had never been exposed to anything like this in her life.

It was getting light out now. They were able to see as they walked even though darkness still loomed through the trees and forest growth on the sides of the path. Bill took the lead and walked swiftly. The wind was whistling through the pines. The remaining dried leaves, low-growing bushes, and plants rustled softly. They could hear small animals, probably squirrels, scurrying around them. Since the larger animals were done for the night, the smaller animals probably felt it was safe to come out now.

When they were in front of the next cabin shortly before the turnoff to the airstrip, they heard a different sound. Someone was coming toward them from Webber's cabin. Whoever it was seemed to be in quite a hurry, because he wasn't trying to mute his footsteps. They could hear leaves crunching at a steady pace.

Bill grabbed Janice's arm and pulled her behind the trunk of a large tree. They turned sideways to shelter themselves as best they could. Fortunately, bushes about four feet tall were in front of the tree. Even though the leaves were completely off the bushes at this time of year, it did provide additional cover for them. They stood absolutely still as the footsteps grew louder. Neither of them knew who it was. Bill bent his arms and held the gun up with one hand wrapped around the other prepared to fire immediately. He surreptitiously looked around the tree.

Janice was terrified. She wanted to pull him back. *Is this it? We're going to be killed out here in the middle of nowhere?* Her eyes bore into him silently screaming don't do that. She watched fascinated as jaw tightened and his nostrils flared out, then his look of caution changed to intense anger.

"Well, well, well. Hello Patrick. Going somewhere?" he asked quietly as he stepped out from behind the tree. He held the gun out in front of him.

For a nanosecond Webber froze, then he turned and began to run down the path to the airstrip. Bill was after him in a shot. He was younger and in better shape and caught up with him before he could run ten yards. He grabbed his arm and spun him around. Webber stumbled but managed to stay on his feet.

Janice sprinted out from the safety of the tree and was a few steps behind Bill as he caught up with Webber. Even she was in better shape than Patrick Webber she noted with some pride. When they met on the path yesterday, she hadn't paid close attention to him. Meeting him up close and face to face, she was surprised at how tall he was. Looking up at him over Bill's shoulder, she was stunned to see there was nothing in his eyes. They were devoid of all emotion. Nothing. The emptiness was the eeriest thing she ever experienced.

With the gun steady and pointed at Webber, Bill did not take his eyes off of him as he spoke to Janice. "We're going to take him back to the shed," Bill said. "Come on, let's go." He nodded his head in the direction of their cabin.

Webber's lips turned into an evil sneer, but his eyes still held nothing. "You have no idea who you're dealing with, Andersen."

"I know exactly who I'm dealing with, you piece of scum. You were planning on making a run for it, weren't you? I'll bet you had the lies all figured out that you're going to tell everyone when you got back to Washington. Well, too late. You're coming with us. Let's go."

Webber raised his chin and looked down on Bill as if he were a piece of garbage, then he sat down on a large rock on the side of the path. "I'm not going anywhere with you. Now what are you going to do about it? Sic the old, lady, guard dog on me?" he snorted as he looked over at Janice. He dismissed her too as if she was of no value.

Janice's eyes became tiny slits. Her nostrils flared. She had never been so angry with another human being in her life. However, when she looked over at Bill to see how he was reacting, she saw that his jaw was clamped shut. He was taking in deep breathes of air through his nose and the hand holding the gun was shaking slightly. *Oh brother. It looks like he wants to kill Webber. If he does, we'll never be able to prove he was the one who planned this whole thing. The press would make it out that Bill was the bad guy. I can't let that happen.* She had to do something. She took a step toward Bill and gently laid her hand on his upper arm. "Bill," she said softly as she reached over with her left hand and put it on his hand holding the gun.

"Give me the gun, Bill," she said. She wanted to say more, but didn't think now was the time for any philosophical discussion.

He blinked several times and gave his head a slight shake like he was coming out of a stupor. He couldn't believe how close he had come to killing another human being. He allowed Janice to take the gun from his hand. But then he noticed Webber was slowly sliding his hand down the side of his leg. He lunged for him and grabbed his arm and held it. He ran his other hand down Webber's pant leg and felt the gun. "Keep your gun on him, Janice. He has a gun in an ankle holster."

Janice walked over to Webber sitting on the rock and knelt down in front of him. She held her gun aimed directly at his heart while Bill retrieved the gun from Webber. It was a tiny stub-nosed pistol. Bill sneered as he put it in his pocket.

Janice couldn't believe it. Webber still had that smarmy smirk on his face. *Time to remove it.* She jammed the barrel of the gun under his chin and forced his head back. No way was she going to look into those hollow orbs of his. She kept her eyes on his nose area. "Okay, asshole. You just ran out of options, because I'm one tough old broad and here's what I'm going to do. I'm going to count to three and if you're not standing and ready to go with us, I'm going to shoot the front of your face off." She pushed on the gun harder and tilted his head back even farther. "It doesn't make any difference if your goons hear the gun shot, because we've got enough guns and ammo back in our cabin to hold off the other two."

"One."

For all Janice's bravado about being 'a tough old broad' and having 'guns and ammo', Bill noticed she was holding the gun by the handle. She didn't even have her finger on the trigger.

"Two."

Bill knew with Webber's head tilted back, he had no way of knowing how Janice was holding it or that it couldn't be fired. So for drama, he said, "Shoot him, Janice. Don't bother counting."

"All right." Webber spat the words out as he started to rise. Bill took his arm and started back down the path to their cabin.

Janice walked behind the men and shoved the gun in his back, again holding on to the handle. She leaned forward. "If you think about trying anything, don't, because this time I won't bother counting to three. I'll just shoot you."

"Both of you are dead," he hissed. "When the people in D.C. hear what you've done, you won't survive 24 hours. You have no idea how many people are involved in this."

"That's a laugh, Webber. Face it. With this screw-up, you're in this alone now," Bill said. "When everyone learns you tried to kidnap me and had plans to have me killed, I'm sure all your *friends* are going to be back pedaling as fast as they can to put distance between themselves and you."

CHAPTER 20

• • •

CARL WAS STILL SITTING IN the recliner but was more awake now. The second dose of pain medicine helped ease the excruciating pain of the beating he received. Peggy and Emily were sitting on the floor of the cabin next to the window. They had pushed the bottom of the lace curtain up about an inch and were keeping watch outside. They felt so vulnerable inside the cabin.

Peggy spotted the trio first. "Oh my god. Bill and Janice have Patrick Webber!"

Emily got up on her knees and peered through the opening to get a better look. "How the hell did that happen?" She went to the door and opened it a crack.

Carl sat up and swung his feet to the side of the chair. "Goo for hem," was all he could say with his jaw still wrapped in the scarf.

As the three walked up the path to the cabin, they could see an eye staring out at them through the crack in the door, and, another eye peeking out of a slit in the front curtains. Other than two eyes showing through the tiny openings, they were unable to tell who was who.

"What the heck happened?" asked the soft voice belonging to the eye at the door. Janice recognized the voice as Emily's.

"Get the tape, and the rope and the key to the shed. Webber's going in there. I'll explain everything when we get inside the shed. Come on hurry. There's still two nut jobs running around out here," Janice said in sotto voice. She and Bill continued to maneuver Webber toward the side of the cabin. As they passed the front windows, she could hear the women scurrying around getting ready to join them. She kept the gun firmly jammed into Patrick's back. She did not want him to get any bright ideas of shouting or trying to escape. They did not need that right now.

When they got to the door of the shed, Bill and Janice turned to check on the progress of the other women. Both were surprised to see that Emily and Peggy had Carl with them. They each held one of his arms supporting him as they approached. Janice noticed he did look much better.

Bill watched the parade as it neared. *Here's one of the richest men in the United States and he's being taken prisoner by three old ladies and beat-up pilot who looks like a lop eared rabbit with the ends of that colorful scarf dangling down along the sides of his head. Someday I'm going to look back on this and laugh . . . but not today.*

While they waited for Peggy to unlock the shed door, Patrick turned and stared at his captors. He was appalled to think, this bunch of yahoos was planning to lock him in a shed. It made him more furious than he had ever been in his life. He knew one thing for certain. When he got out of this mess, he would make sure every one of them ended up dead. But he had to get out of here. He couldn't be caught. "All right. How much money do you want? I can pay each of you a half a million dollars to let me go."

With a look of pure disgust as if he had just swallowed a rotten egg, Bill said nothing, but just shook his head at the man.

The way Carl was trussed up, he could do little more than glare at him.

Peggy swung the door open and swept her hand toward the shed like a doorman on Park Avenue. "Good try, but no thanks. Get inside."

Janice nudged him with the gun. "Come on, let's go."

Emily just snorted. "You kidnapped the Vice President and planned to kill him, and the only thing you think will get you out of this mess is money. Your cupidity has really made you stupid, Webber." She gave him a shove.

Even though the sun was now just over the horizon, it was still somewhat dark in the cabin. It wasn't until he entered and grew accustomed to the gloom that Patrick saw one of his men taped up and lying on the floor. His head jerked back, and he sucked in a quick breath of air. "If you think you idiots are going to tie me up like that, think again, assholes," He twisted and ran for the door while he shouted, "Help!"

Everything seemed to happen at once. Webber plowed into Emily and knocked her on her keister. Bill tried to grab his arm as he ran passed, but Webber flipped it up and Bill lost his grip. Carl wedged himself into a corner not wanting to be involved in any more pain. Ever the planner, Peggy slammed the door shut impeding Webber's exit then grabbed a shovel leaning against the wall next to the door. She didn't swing it, knowing it wouldn't work in the confines of the shed filled with people. She merely heaved it forward. The end of the shovel smacked Webber right in the middle of his stomach and knocked the wind out of him. That respite allowed Bill to grab him from behind and pull him back to the middle of the shed.

By this time, Emily had gotten off the floor, regaining some of her dignity for landing on her *tuckus*, and had the duct tape out. She tore off a piece and slapped it across Webber's mouth cutting off any more shouting antics.

Rattled, Janice just stood there still holding the gun. During the melee it never occurred to her to try to use it. With all the people flying around, she probably would have missed Webber and hit one of the others. She looked around for Carl. "Carl, are you okay?" she called out.

He stepped out of the gloom of the corner. As he slowly walked into the lighter area of the shed, with one eye shut and mouth still swollen, his arm in a sling and the scarf ends dangling down his head, he looked like a monster emerging from the depths in a B-movie horror film. "Here," he answered.

Peggy's fuse blew. She had had it. Still holding the shovel, she stomped over to the group and got up into Webber's face. She poked the shovel into his side. "Enough! Get down on your knees right now or so help me, I'll flatten you with this shovel." There must have been a tone in her voice or a look in her eye. Webber knelt. She turned to the rest of the group. "Get him tied up and check his pockets for a phone."

Emily went to work taping his wrists behind his back and then started on his ankles. When she was done, she put the tape back in her jacket. Bill patted him down and found a cell phone in his pants pocket. He shoved the phone in his jacket pocket. "The FBI is going to have a field day getting into this phone." When they were finished Emily and Bill stood up.

Webber was seated on the floor with his wrists bound behind him. "That's not going to work," Bill said. "He'll be able to stand and move around." He took a few moments to look around the shed. "Peggy, hand me one of those paddles. Emily, how much rope is left?"

Peggy leaned over the other man lying along the side of the canoe and retrieved a paddle. Bill took it, knelt down and slid it through Webber's arms along his back. Webber made a feeble attempt to resist until Peggy gave him a good kick in the hip.

"With the paddle stuck through his arms, he won't be able to roll over," Bill said. "Now for the rope." He took the remaining rope Emily had cut away from the canoe and threaded a few feet of it between Webber's right arm and side and wrapped it around the end the paddle sticking out. Then he hauled the end along the back of Webber and brought it through Webber's left arm and side. He also wrapped it around the end of the paddle on that side. He took the two ends of the rope and tied them around Webber's feet in a secure knot. "There that should hold him until the military gets here."

Janice thought Webber looked like a trussed up Thanksgiving turkey. "As long as you have a phone, do you want to go make your call to the White House, Bill?"

Bill started for the door. "No. I still need to make sure my Secret Service agent is okay. Right now that's my number one priority. With two men still running around, I think we have to move fast. Come on let's go back to the cabin and talk."

Bill slowly opened the door and reconnoitered. He didn't want to walk out straight into the arms of the other men. The area up to the cabin looked clear. Right before he nodded his head to the others indicating they should follow him, he put his finger to his lips for silence. Emily and Janice took Carl. Peggy finally put the shovel down against the wall and locked the shed as she was leaving. They heard nothing on their way to the cabin.

CHAPTER 21

• • •

ONCE INSIDE, BILL IMMEDIATELY TOOK charge. The trauma of the past twenty-four hours was wearing off. He felt more in control of himself, better able to think and plan. "From now on we need to stick together. Carl, how you feeling? Think you can go with us?"

"Yeah, mush better," he answered.

"Good. I don't want to leave any of you alone in this cabin anymore. We have pushed our luck as far as we can for meeting up with the two remaining men. We caught two, but that doesn't mean we can catch the other two as successfully. So here's the plan. First, we go down to the airstrip and rescue my agent then we make the call to the White House. Once that's done, we'll try to find a hiding place and wait for help to arrive." He looked around and waited for their reply.

"Sounds good."

"I like it."

"No hiding. Ah can fly you out a here," Carl said.

Jaws dropped, four sets of eyes zeroed in on Carl. For a moment no one said a word.

"Carl," Janice began. "You still have one eye completely swollen shut. Your arm is in a sling. I doubt you can even raise it three inches without extreme pain in your ribs. I'm sorry, love, but there is no way you are in any shape to fly a plane."

"Janice is right, Carl. Physically, you're in no condition to fly a plane," Bill added. "Thanks for the offer, but don't worry. We'll find someplace to be safe."

What about getting the pilots on Webber's plane to fly us out of here?" Janice asked.

Peggy shook her head. "That's not a good idea, because we don't know if the pilots are in on the plot to kidnap Bill or not. They could easily fly all of us out of the country, and we wouldn't know."

Everyone was silent for a moment. Emily took a step forward. "Peggy and I can fly Carl's plane and get us out of here." Emily said quietly. She cringed at the cacophony of shouting coming from everyone all at once.

"What?"

"What?"

"Waa?"

"What!!!"

The loudest "what" was uttered by Peggy. She stood looking at Emily with her mouth hanging open. Her eyes were so wide open both irises were completely exposed. Bewilderment, agony, confusion, and terror played across her face like a piano arpeggio. With jaw clamped shut, Emily glared back at her through squinted eyes desperately trying to silently command her not to say a word.

"Mah plane," Carl moaned as he sat down on a kitchen chair.

"Look, Peggy and I have been flying planes for years. You know that, Janice," she said looking first at Janice in innocence and without a smidge of guile and then over at Peggy with another warning shot across the bow look of *keep your mouth shut*. "We both have our pilot's license for a twin-engine plane." She turned to Bill. "As soon as we get your agent out of the jet, you hurry over and get on Carl's plane so we can fly everyone out of here. I don't want to wander around looking for a safe place to hide, Bill. You're right, we've taken care of two of the men, but the odds are against us taking care of the other two. We only have the one decent size gun we took off the beefcake, and that tiny pop-gun you found on Webber will probably be useless. How long will we be able to hold off the other two with those – no matter where we hide?"

Bill rubbed a hand over his face. "So far you women really proved to be invaluable. I wouldn't be standing here if it wasn't for you. You were the ones who subdued the goon this morning, and were like professionals with Webber and his antics in the shed. But getting on a plane with Emily and Peggy as pilots . . . that scares the hell out of me."

Emily winced at Bill's words, and it didn't help that Peggy was glaring at her with that *I told you so* look.

"Emily's right," Janice interjected. "I think we've really pushed the envelope standing around here. Sooner or later one of those men roaming around is going to find us. I can keep myself together for only so long. The last twenty-four hours have been surreal enough. Thank you very much." She looked at Bill and Carl. "I've flown with Emily a number of times. She and Peggy are more than capable of getting us out of here. Now come on. Let's go get that agent of yours, Bill. I'll help you, and while you and I are doing that, Emily and Peggy can get Carl settled in the other plane and start on their pre-flight work." She patted her pockets checking for the gun, Emily's knife and the duct tape. "When we get him free, we can tape up the two pilots."

Listening to the women, it finally dawned on Bill that the three of them had been ordering him around and making all the decisions ever since Emily first peeked into the window of Webber's shed. *When did I lose control of the situation? Did I ever have control? I am the Vice President of the United States! I'm next in line for the Presidency, for crying out loud. Yet these three women are ordering me around like a fifth grader!*

Before Bill could even finish his musings, the women already had Carl up and out of the chair and were standing at the door waiting for him. *I don't believe this. Like a dummy, I going to do what they want. They make my old, Marine Drill Sergeant seem like a wuss.*

"Listen," Emily said before she opened the door. "Janice, you and Bill take Carl and help him. Peggy and I will bring up the rear." She slowly opened the door inch by inch while she inspected the surroundings. She didn't see anyone lurking around and couldn't hear any leaves crunching. "Okay, let's go," she whispered. The five of them scooted down to the path in front of the cabin and turned north. Because the sun was now fully over the horizon they had no trouble seeing the path.

At the first opportunity of being out of hearing range, Peggy grabbed Emily's arm. "So, just when were you going to tell the others even though we've had our single-engine pilot's licenses for years, you and I only got our twin-engine pilot's license a mere 30 days ago?" she hissed. "No way are we flying that plane, you fool."

"Hey," Emily said as she disengaged her arm from Peggy's firm grasp. "It doesn't matter how long we've had our license. What matters is, we took all the classes, flew the plane with an instructor and passed the Checkride to earn our certificate. You and I can fly that plane, Peggy. After what we've been through in less than twenty-four hours, there is no way I'm staying here to be shot at. Good grief, we've got the Vice President to protect. We can't stay running around trying to find a hidey-hole until help arrives."

Peggy threw her hands up. "Do you realize all the things that could go wrong?" she asked. "For crying out loud, Emily, you and I are going to be flying with the Vice President of the United States on board."

"We'll fly to Missoula. It has a traffic control tower. Once we radio just who we've got on board, they can guide us in. Up, down, it should only take us about 30 minutes."

"Emily, I'm terrified."

Emily rolled her eyes. "You think I'm not?"

Peggy opened her mouth to speak, then stopped with her head down and her shoulders drooping. It took her a moment then she slowly shook her head and whispered, "All right, I'll do it."

CHAPTER 22

• • •

THE FIVE OF THEM STOOD behind large boulders and scanned the airstrip. They didn't see either of the men with the guns. However, the co-pilot of the corporate jet was outside inspecting the plane. It looked like he was going through the pre-flight preparation. With all the high-tech stuff on the roof of his cabin, Webber must have been able to contact them and told them to get the plane ready for take-off. The side door was open and the steps were down. The engines of the jet had not been started yet. All seemed quiet.

The jet and Carl's plane had pulled completely off the runway after they had landed yesterday, and were now parked along the side of it on the grass. The jet was parked on the left with the nose facing away from them. Carl's plane was on the right and slightly behind the jet.

"Janice, you go with the others and get on Carl's plane. I'll get Agent Daniels myself," Bill said to the group.

"Don't be ridicules, Bill," Janice whispered. "Those pilots know who you are. The minute you step out of here and they see you, they'll slam the door shut and take off. You'll never know where your Agent is."

Ugh. She's doing this to me again!

"I'm going to sneak farther down and come out of the bushes yelling for help. I'll say my friend fell and broke her leg. That should get the co-pilot's attention." She turned to Bill. "Then you sneak up from this side and grab him and use Webber's gun. The pilot in the plane shouldn't be able to see what's going on out here when you grab him. You still have Webber's gun, don't you?"

Bill nodded.

She turned to the other three. "Once Bill and I are in the jet, you two hurry up and get Carl to the other plane and start your pre-flight stuff, okay?" Emily and Peggy nodded their heads in agreement. With that she turned and scurried through the brush and behind boulders to get in position.

Before Bill could voice any objections, Janice was already half way to the jet. He had no choice. He followed Janice.

Janice came running out in the open waving her arms wildly and yelling "Help! Help!" She tried to stay slightly to the right of the front window, because she didn't want the inside pilot to be able to see what was taking place out here. The co-pilot jerked around when he heard her shouts for help.

"You've got to help me. My friend is over there," she said pointing behind her and to the left. She wanted him to face away from the body of the plane so he wouldn't see Bill sneaking up behind him.

"What happened, Lady?" he asked her. Alarmed, he began walking toward her.

"We were hiking and my friend fell down and she can't get up!" *I can't believe I just said that.*

The tail of the jet was high enough so Bill merely had to lower his head as he came around and grabbed the co-pilot from behind and shove the gun in his neck. "Don't make a sound," he said quietly in the guy's ear.

The gun in his neck and a little, blond old lady yelling for help did not belong together. "What the hell is this?" the pilot asked. He managed to turn his head. He realized it was the Vice President holding him captive! This confused him because Patrick Webber had not shared his kidnap plans with either of his pilots. They were only told to keep an eye on the Secret Service Agent they were holding because he went rogue.

Janice walked over to the men and pulled out the gun she took from Bill earlier in the day. She pointed it at the co-pilot. "We've come to get the Vice President's Secret Service Agent. Where is he?"

Oh, this is just great. Janice is standing there with a gun the size of a Howitzer and me macho, ex-Marine, am standing here with this itty-bitty pop-gun. I bet if I pulled the trigger, it would just go "pfft" and squeeze out a bullet. The only thing that would happen to the pilot is he'd have a pockmark on his neck. Jeez. This is so embarrassing. He needed to get some of his dignity back. "Enough, Janice. We need to get on the jet before the other pilot is aware of what's happening." He pushed the co-pilot toward the open door of the plane.

CHAPTER 23

• • •

THE MINUTE EMILY AND PEGGY saw Janice and Bill walk the pilot toward the jet, they took Carl and scooted out from behind the boulders and hurried to his plane. Peggy opened the door and let down the steps. Emily went first. At the top, she turned around and grabbed Carl's jacket pulling him up the steps while Peggy pushed him from behind. They got him seated in one of the passenger seats.

"I can fly plane," Carl kept repeating over and over. He even tried to rise out of his seat. Peggy put her arm on his shoulder and gently sat him back down and buckled his seat belt.

"You can't Carl," she said softly in his ear. He slumped in the seat. She patted his arm. "Don't worry, we'll take good care of your plane. We've flown this type of plane numerous times." She winced as she made up the part about numerous times.

Emily went to the front and got into the pilot's seat and strapped herself in. She scanned the instrument panel. It looked just like the one on the other twin-engine she and Peggy flew to get their licenses for which she was very grateful. She pulled out the pre-flight checklist.

"Carl's all taken care of. I'll go do the outside checks," Peggy said. "But before I go, let's look at that GPS map and figure out which airport to fly to." She sat in the co-pilot's seat and turned on the computer GPS map located in the middle part of the control panel within easy reach of both pilots. They scanned it and concluded the Missoula Airport was indeed their best bet, because it had an air-traffic control tower. The Stevensville airport was much closer, but it did not have a control tower. Fortunately, according to the map if they flew slightly to the west after take-off, they would be able to fly up a valley between two sets of mountain ranges straight into Missoula.

Even though the actual flight would be less than 30 minutes in duration, the women checked the weather between Burnt Fork Lake and Missoula. Things looked calm and holding, no huge snowstorms coming out of the Rockies from the west.

"Everything looks good, Peggy. When the pre-flight check is over, we're good to take off." She looked out the side window and didn't see any movement around the jet yet. "I hope things are okay over there. Do you want to take a walk over and see if something is wrong?"

"No. Give it a few more minutes. I'll go outside and get started on the outside checking. Keep an eye out for Janice and Bill. Once you see them come out, file our flight plan with Missoula, and be sure to tell them the Vice President is on board. That should clear the skies and open all the runways when we land. I still don't think we should . . . " Peggy shook her head and stared out the front window. "Aw, forget it." She flapped her hand in resignation as she got out of the co-pilot's seat and started for the door.

CHAPTER 24

• • •

ONCE AGAIN, SOMEHOW JANICE OUT maneuvered Bill and managed to enter the plane first. She had the gun held in front of her. Bill was shaking his head in frustration as he and the co-pilot boarded behind her. The inside pilot turned in his seat and stood up when he saw them. He stopped where he was when he saw the guns. Bill and Janice spotted Agent Daniels taped and gagged and sitting in the front passenger seat. Both were so relieved he was still alive.

With her gun, Janice motioned for the pilot to come into the compartment. ""Sorry about this guys, but we can't let you fly out of here. Come over here and sit down," she ordered. Agent Daniels watched Janice wave the gun around. If by some miracle he got free, he'd take the old lady down. He had to protect the Vice President, but when he looked back at the Vice President, he seemed calm and reserved as he led the co-pilot forward.

"What are you doing? Where's Mr. Webber?" the pilot asked.

"He won't be here. He's a bit tied up at the moment," Janice answered with a straight face. "We're going to tape you up so you can't fly out of here. But don't worry, someone will be here by this afternoon to free you." Neither pilot understood Janice's cryptic message.

When the pilots were seated, Janice padded her pockets until she located the knife. She took it out, held it up and pushed the button on the side. *Snick.* Out popped a four-inch blade. Both pilots and Bill's Agent jerked in their seats waiting to see just what it was she intended to do with it. She simply handed it to Bill while she padded her pockets looking for the duct tape. "Here, use this to free your Agent," she said in a commanding voice. She kept her gun pointed at the pilots. "I'll keep an eye on these two while you free him."

Bill cut the tape binding his Agent's wrists and bent down to free his legs. The minute his hands were free, Agent Daniels ripped the tape off his mouth and stood up. He almost knocked Bill over, but he wasn't prepared for the pain shooting across his face from the pulled tape. He stumbled back into his seat and began rubbing his mouth and cheeks until the burning sensation subsided somewhat.

"Mr. Vice President, are you okay?"

"Yeah, Phil. I'm fine."

Agent Daniels looked over at Janice holding the gun and gave a quick jerk of his head toward her. "What's with the old lady and the gun?" he asked out of the side of his mouth.

"Hey! I heard that 'old lady' remark, kiddo." Janice said. Her eyes were slits as she looked at him.

Bill smiled. "I'll explain everything when we get out of here. Come on we have to secure these two pilots. By-the-way, where's your phone, Phil?"

Daniels had been bound in a sitting position for so long, as he stood he had to shake his arms and legs trying to get the circulation back. "They took it. Its up in the cockpit."

"Go get it," Bill said as he took the tape from Janice and began binding the pilots.

They were just finished with the binding of the men's wrists to the armrests and their feet to the seat legs when Daniels brought his phone back. Bill reached for it. "Is it charged? Can I make a call?" Agent Daniels nodded.

"Help Janice finish up with these guys, Phil" he said handing over the spool of the tape.

Bill closed his eyes for a split second and smiled briefly as relief of being able to contact the White House washed over him. He dialed the special number and gave the special code to indicate he was in extreme danger.

As soon as Bill gave the special code, without waiting to hear another word, the Agent in Washington who took Bill's call opened the computer program developed after 9-11 and pressed *enter*. Within nano-seconds alerts went out worldwide. Bill's phone call was now not only being monitored, but his words were automatically translated into text based on voice recognition. That verbatim text simultaneously appeared on the "hot" screens of the Pentagon and the command centers of the Army, Navy, Air Force, Marines and Coast Guard. The text also went to the President's phone and the command centers of the Secret Service, C.I.A., Homeland Security, NSA and the F.B.I. A special general alert, without details, was sent to the State Department and every United States Embassy throughout the world. Within minutes, Secret Service Agents were being assembled to locate and then sent to guard the people in succession to the Presidency – the Speaker of the House, the President pro tempore of the Senate and the Secretary of State. An additional Secret Service detail surrounded the President.

Even though Agent Daniels no longer had his weapon, his partner, Agent Kovac took it from him before he left the jet yesterday afternoon, when he heard the Vice President utter the code, he immediately moved and stood next to him in a protective mode.

Bill relayed the facts of being kidnapped by Patrick Webber, being rescued, the location of Webber, his two pilots and one of his henchmen, freeing Agent Daniels and the betrayal of Agent Kovac. He remained a bit hazy on the details of the ages of his rescuers and how they managed to subdue Webber and the other man. Who would believe him? Once he was assured the White House was able to locate him through GPS, he asked how long it would be for help to arrive. He explained there were two armed men still at large. He held off on letting Washington know there was another plane available to fly everyone out. Emily and Peggy at the helm still made him nervous.

The two pilots stared in horror when they heard what the Vice President said. They had no idea what their boss intended to do when they flew the people up here. "Hey, we had no part in the kidnapping. You've got to believe us."

Agent Daniels had been an Agent for fifteen years and was a member of the elite Secret Service detail in the White House. He could not believe what he was hearing either. As an Agent he felt such guilt for not being able to stop the kidnapping. He knew he would carry that guilt with him for the rest of his life.

Of the four of them only Janice looked over at Bill and gave him big grin and a thumbs-up. It was easy to do, because she and Emily and Peggy had been involved with everything that had happened.

When he paused in his narrative, Janice said, "Bill, I don't think we should waste any more time. We need to get on the other plane and get out of here. Can you walk and talk at the same time?" She took in a breath of air and wrinkled her nose as she realized the walk and talk barb. She waved her hand and said, "You know what I mean."

Agent Daniels swiveled his head back and forth between the Vice President and Janice. "What plane?" he demanded.

"A plane?" came a voice on the phone.

Bill grimaced as if he were in extreme pain. "Ah, yeah . . . there's a twin-engine plane ready to fly us out of here," he said to the person in Washington.

CHAPTER 25

• • •

WHILE EMILY WAS DOING THE pre-flight, she took a moment to look out the front window to survey the surroundings. Since they were sitting in a valley, she wanted to understand what she would have to do on the take-off. The actual high mountains were far in the distance. They posed no problem, because there would be plenty of time to reach the necessary altitude to fly above them. However, all her previous take-offs were done at airports that were surrounded by flat land. She was always able to bring the plane up slowly. Here, looking down the runway, the real problem on take-off was going to be the hills that rose up shortly after the end of the runway. She estimated they wouldn't have much room from the end of the runway before the smaller hills would force the plane into a rapid ascent, and what made it worse was the tall pine trees growing on the top of those hills. She would definitely have to get the plane into a steep climb the minute the wheels left the ground. One good thing in her favor was the plane wasn't loaded down with baggage. There was less weight so it wouldn't require a higher speed to get liftoff. Looking down the runway, she figured the plane would have wheels up when it was about three-quarters of the way down. That should give her plenty of time to put the plane into a steep ascent in order to skim above the top of those trees. She knew it would not be easy, but she and Peggy had practiced short field takeoffs a number of times during training. Now it was time to start the on-board pre-flight check, but before she did, she took one last look down the runway. She scrunched up her face and pursed her lips. Something didn't seem right and it had nothing to do with the quick ascent she would have to make. *Maybe it's an optical illusion of being in a valley surrounded by the hills and trees that's making me uncomfortable,* she thought. She gave her head a small shake to bring her out of her musings. She had things to do.

While Peggy was checking the wheel wells, she spotted Janice, Bill and another man come out of the jet. *Good. Looks like they got Bill's Agent and he's okay.* Bill was speaking on a phone. *Thank goodness. Bet he's in contact with the White House and help is on the way. Maybe we won't have to fly out of here.*

After he heard the Vice President tell Washington there was another plane available to fly them out, Agent Daniels took one look at the twin-engine plane sitting across the tarmac and said, "No way, Mr. Vice President. No way, am I going to allow you on that plane. It looks old, and it hasn't been checked out by our Secret Service plane detail."

"Phil, there are six of us, one has been injured and can hardly walk. There are still two men out there with automatic weapons. We won't be able to stay hidden for long before they find us. This plane is our best bet on getting out of here."

"Besides, we've already talked it over and the decision has been made to fly out of here," Janice nodded and added her two cents. She was still holding the gun along the side of her.

Daniels fuse was burning low. He wasn't able to prevent the kidnapping. He was kept prisoner in the jet. The Vice President didn't seem to be listening to him, and now this old lady was in his face. He looked down at her gun. "Give me that gun, Lady."

Janice almost had to take a step back when he referred to her as "lady".

"No," she told him. Actually, after Bill got on the plane, she planned on staying outside to protect Peggy while she did her checking. She needed that gun.

"I am the Secret Service Agent for the Vice President of the United States. I want that gun . . .now!"

"Ah . . . Phil." Bill was quite sure he knew where this would lead.

"In your dreams, Buddy," Janice snarled as she turned and began walking to the plane. "You need to get Bill on that plane."

"Hey! I said give me the gun," Daniels reached out and grabbed Janice's arm and spun her around and tried to grab the gun out of her hand. She pulled her arm out of his reach.

Although she couldn't hear what was being said, Peggy saw what was happening to her friend. She stomped over to help her. "Hey, Bozo, what do you think you're doing," she shouted.

"Phil, don't do that. You can have my gun," Bill said not realizing the phone he was holding was still on.

"Mr. Vice President! What's happening? What gun? Are you okay?" came the Washington voice. Bill rolled his eyes and groaned inwardly.

Just then Peggy arrived. She put hands on the Agent's chest and gave him a shove. He lost hold of Janice's arm and stumbled backwards.

Janice switched the gun to her left hand and swung with her right, a real round-house, and socked Agent Daniels in the upper arm.

"Ouch!" he said as he grabbed his arm where she hit him. It hurt. For being an old lady she really packed a wallop.

"Enough!" yelled the Vice President. "Janice, Peggy . . . knock it off. Phil, we are getting on that plane. You can have my gun," Bill said. Janice and Peggy became very still. In just those few sentences with that tone in his voice, they realized what the power of the Vice President of the United States was really all about.

"But, Mr. Vice President," Agent Daniels tried one more time. "The plane hasn't been checked out. We don't know what condition it's in."

Bill took the snub-nose out of his pocket and handed it to his Agent. "Here take this."

Daniels just looked at the puny gun being offered. "You've got to be kidding. What did you do? Get this out of a Cracker Jack box? And what am I supposed to do? Say bang when I pull the trigger?"

"It was Webber's gun." Bill had had enough. He started toward the plane. "Let's go."

Peggy walked along with Bill back to the plane to finish the outside pre-check. Janice stayed behind and kept an eye on the surroundings.

CHAPTER 26

• • •

ONCE EMILY SAW BILL AND Janice and the other man, whom she assumed was his Agent, exit the jet, she turned forward in her seat and flipped a switch to turn on the radio to make contact with the Missoula air-traffic control. After she identified Carl's plane and filed her flight plan, she informed the person in Missoula that they would be flying with the Vice President on board and requested all runways be cleared for landing.

"Cessna 14590 repeat message. The Vice President of the United States is on board your plane?" came the return voice of the controller.

Emily knew this wasn't going to be easy. "This is an emergency and we will be flying with Vice President, Bill Andersen on board. Suggest you clear all runways for landing."

"Is this a joke?" the man asked in a monotone voice. During his years as a controller, he had heard it all from drunken pilots trying to land on the wrong runway to having to talk down planes in serious mechanical trouble. But this was a first and he wasn't amused. However, he needn't have bothered getting worked up. Just then a national emergency alert flashed on all traffic control screens in the tower, because when Peggy heard Bill talking on the phone to Washington informing them they were not going to wait for help to arrive, but were going to fly out of Burnt Fork Lake, she told him it was decided they would be flying into Missoula. He relayed the message to Washington. Again, as with his original emergency code message, the person in Washington opened another computer program to the National Air Traffic Control Center informing them of the Vice President's location and flight destination. Within seconds, alerts went out to control towers in seven northwest states. Planes immediately started to be diverted away from Montana, and planes at the Missoula airport were stopped from taking off and required to return to the terminals until further notice. Along with public airports, air force jet pilots at the Malmstrom Air Force Base in Montana were ordered to gear up and be ready to take off on command.

The veteran controller in Missoula quickly relayed the flight plan and message to the National Air Traffic Control Center that the Vice President would be on board Cessna 14590 flying out of Burnt Fork Lake. Nothing like this had ever happened at the Missoula Airport. The people in the control tower were ecstatic.

Someone in the control tower called the T.V. news stations to alert them to what was about to happen.

● ● ●

When they entered the plane, Agent Daniels remained standing in the aisle. "Mr. Vice President who the hell is that lady in the pilot's seat? Where's the pilot?"

"He's sitting over there, Phil," Bill pointed to Carl. "He was beaten by Webber's men and is in no condition to fly this plane." He nodded his head to the front. "That's Emily. She and her friend, Peggy, will be flying us out."

"Are you kidding? Those old ladies are older than Methuselah's grandmother, for crying out loud."

Bill smiled. "That may be, but those three old ladies are the ones who rescued Carl and me last night. I'll tell you about it later."

While Emily had been going through the pre-flight inside check list, she noticed one of her gloves had fallen out of her jacket pocket and was on the floor next to her seat. She bent down to retrieve it. In that brief moment as she was bent over, because everything in the outer shell of this plane was plastic, she heard – "Pop . . . whiz . . . pop".

"What was that noise?" she asked coming up upright in her seat, it was then she noticed a small round hole in her side window and another one in the co-pilot's window. "Good grief!" she yelled. "We're being shot at!" The muscles in her body seemed frozen. She couldn't move, but thoughts were swirling in her head. *I could have been killed. Should I duck down? Who's shooting at us? Now what do I do? Where's Peggy and Janice? Are they okay?*

When Emily announced they were being shot at, Agent Daniels immediately pounced on top of the Vice President. Maybe he couldn't prevent him from being kidnapped, but no way was he going to allow anything else to happen to him. While on top of him, he pulled the tiny snub-nose gun out of his pocket. "Shit" was his only remark as he looked at it in his hand.

Bill was bent over the armrest and couldn't breathe with his Agent on top of him. "Get off of me, Phil," he tried to shout. The words came out muffled under Daniels' body, but he must have heard something, because Daniels eased up a bit and took some of his weight off Bill.

Peggy rushed into the plane. "They found us. Get those engines started, Emily. We've got to get ready to get out of here."

"Where's Janice?"

"She's still outside shooting at them. She told me to get in here and get the plane started."

"What do you mean, she's shooting at them. She doesn't even own a gun!"

"Well, you wouldn't know it by looking at her, because when she realized the guy was firing his gun, she instantly dropped to the ground and started firing back. She looked just like a Biathlon Cross Country Skier in the Winter Olympics, for crying out loud."

Peggy plopped down in the co-pilot's seat. "Start those engines, damn it." She reached over and pushed Engine #1 and then Engine #2. The propellers turned slowly at first and then got in sync and spun at full idle.

Agent Daniels was still covering Bill. His head jerked up when Peggy came barreling into the plane and went to the front. His mouth fell open and terror swept over his face. He looked down at Bill. "Please don't tell me she's the co-pilot."

Bill raised his head and looked around Daniels' shoulder at Peggy. "Yeah," he said. "That's Methuselah's grandmother's sister."

"Son of a bitch," Daniels muttered.

Peggy looked down the runway. "What the hell's with that runway? Where are all the markings?" she asked.

No markings. That's it! That's what had been bothering me about this runway, Emily thought.

During the simulation classes and all the airports she and Peggy actually flew into and out of, there were always markings on the runways. This runway had none.

On a marked runway, it begins with threshold markings or "piano keys". They are long, thin, white rectangular lines. Depending on the number of keys, they indicate the width of the runway. They also indicate the no landing zone, since that part of the runway isn't strong enough to sustain a plane landing.

The number of the runway appears above the threshold markings. The number must be six feet in height. The numbers are based on a 360 degree circle to indicate the direction of landings or take-offs. They are written in shorthand compass degrees. The zero is dropped. For example, if a plane is coming in on runway 09 (the other end will be marked with a 27), this indicates an east/west direction – 90 degrees and 270 degrees on the circle. If the runway is marked 18 (the other end will be marked with a 36), this indicates a south/north direction – 180 degrees and 360 degrees on the circle.

The touchdown zone where the runway is stronger and can sustain a landing comes above the number. . It is marked with shorter, wider, rectangles. A plane should touchdown on these markings to ensure there is enough distance remaining on the runway for a safe landing. The broken, centerline running down the middle of the runway begins between the touchdown markers. The centerline serves as a focal point for the nose of the plane on take-offs and landings.

Then various smaller rectangles appear on each side of the centerline to indicate the number of feet remaining to the end of the runway.

Emily looked down the barren runway and swallowed. Oh boy, it wasn't the beginning markers she was worried about. It was the various markings after the touchdown zone. How are we going to know how many feet are left until the end, she thought. She turned her head and looked at the windows.

"What do we do about the bullet holes in the windows?" she pointed to the two windows. "The minute we get airborne, we won't have any inside air pressure. Even though the windows are plastic, I'm sure they'll shatter before we even level out."

"I told you something would happen," Peggy muttered more to herself than Emily. She ran her hand over the hole in her window and then leaned forward and examined Emily's window. "Give me the duct tape."

Emily reached into her pocket. "You think that will hold?" she asked handing the tape to her friend.

Peggy shrugged her shoulders. "It's all we've got, isn't it?" She ripped off strips and began to tape the hole on her side. First, she used two, four-inch strips to make a cross over the hole, then she used the next two to make an "X". She stood up, leaned across and did the same thing to Emily's window. When done, they could barely see out the side windows now covered with the flower patterned duct tape.

"I hope Janice is okay," Emily said. "We can't see very much out these side windows, but the shooting seems to have stopped."

"When I got on the plane, she was lying on the ground about twenty feet behind the tail firing away." Peggy said a silent prayer as they waited for Janice to return. *Please let her be safe, Lord.*

CHAPTER 27

• • •

WHILE JANICE HAD BEEN SCANNING the area waiting for Peggy to finish her outside inspection, she spotted Bill's other Agent come out from behind a boulder across the field about fifty yards away. He had two guns, one in each hand. With the gun in his right hand, he aimed and shot at the plane. She heard the pop, pop as the bullet hit the front of it. First she shouted to Peggy to get back on the plane, and then she immediately fell to the ground and lay there in a prone position, arms out in front, elbows bent with the gun held in both hands. By this time, the Agent was running parallel to the plane. She realized he was trying to get behind the wing so he could shoot a hole in the gas tank. Apparently, his first shot didn't do any major damage.

Janice lowered her head to the gun sight and took aim, just like her instructor at the gun range taught her to do. She followed the Agent as he ran and then fired one shot. Bam! Her bullet hit him in the upper right leg. The sudden pain caused him to drop the gun in his left hand. He still tried to go forward now dragging his right leg. When he grabbed the leg with his right hand still holding the remaining gun, it went off. It looked like he shot himself in the foot. He dropped that gun, staggered forward, and then fell to the ground in agony.

A sneer slide across Janice's face when she saw what he had done to himself. *Good, you creep. You deserve that.*

Higher up on the hill behind where the Agent was writhing in pain, Webber's beefcake came running down the hill. He was zig-zagging between the trees and boulders all the while firing off his automatic. Trying to be macho, he looked like a ham actor in a Hollywood shoot-um-up action movie where all the actors on screen shoot off hundreds of bullets, but hit nothing. Because of his unsteadiness, his bullets flew uselessly to the left, the right, and up in the air. Finally, with all his shenanigans, he emptied his gun. That's when Janice took aim, pulled the trigger and hit him in the shoulder. He dropped his empty gun, grabbed his arm and ran back up into the hills. He didn't even try to help Bill's wounded Agent. *Not true. There really is no honor among thieves.*

She looked back at the Agent on the ground. He was still writhing in pain and didn't look to be a problem anymore, but she waited a few more moments just to be sure. When he began to drag himself back to the trees without trying to retrieve either of the guns, she rose and ran to the door of the plane. The backwash of the rotating propellers impeded her progress. She had to fight her way to the steps, and literally had to crawl the few remaining feet and then up the steps into the plane.

"Help me pull the stairs up," she shouted at no one in particular.

Agent Daniels responded, and the two of them got the steps up and folded. They didn't have to worry about closing the door. The minute the steps were up, the propeller back wash, slammed the door shut. Daniels merely had to reach over and secure the latch.

Janice handed him the gun. "Here. You can have this now. Better check to see if there are any bullets left. There might be one or two, but I doubt it." He took the gun and scowled at her.

The front seat behind the pilots was empty. Janice headed for it. "Both of the bad guys went back into the woods. Get us out of here," she yelled over the roar of the engines.

Emily turned the nose of the plane to the runway. "I didn't know you own a gun?" she shouted back at Janice.

"Are you kidding? You know me better than that. I would never own a gun."

"Well, where the hell did you learn to shoot like that?"

"Oh, that. Well, I wanted to know what guns were all about, so I took lessons," Janice said. "Good thing I did too." She scowled as she looked at the two side windows in the pilot's area. "I take it the duct tape on the windows is where Bill's agent got us. Will the holes affect air pressure?"

By this time Peggy and Emily had the plane situated on the runway and were revving up the engines for takeoff. Neither bother answering Janice's question about the air pressure, both were completely engaged in getting the plane airborne.

Emily pushed the throttle forward and released the brakes. The plane began to move and pick up speed quickly. The flaps were extended slightly to give it the necessary lift. Yet, as the plane picked up speed, Emily thought the end of the runway was coming up way too fast.

"Ah . . . Does this runway seem short to you?" she asked Peggy while keeping her eyes straight ahead. "The runways we've taken off from seemed longer." Emily pushed the throttle forward for more speed. Even with that, the plane did not begin to fly itself yet. The wheels stayed firmly on the ground. She was desperately waiting for the brief moment when the plane flew itself so she could pull back on the yoke and get it up.

Peggy checked the position of the wings. They were extended where they should be. She looked out the front window and was appalled at how quickly they were coming up to the end of the runway. "We've got to get this plane up, Emily," she shouted. On every take off the two of them had made previously, there was always more than enough runway, but not this one. This one was shorter.

"Tell me something I don't know," was Emily's reply. She increased the speed one more time. "Come on. Start flying, damn it," she uttered under her breath. There couldn't have been more than 30 or 40 feet of runway left!

This was it. They were streaking to the very end. Emily knew at this speed, she wouldn't be able to stop the plane. They were going to crash directly into the boulders looming in front of them. However, just as the nose of the plane crossed the very end of the runway, they felt that indescribable feeling of the plane lifting ever so slightly off the ground. It was flying itself! The wheels skimmed the top of the grass. Emily quickly pulled the yoke toward her. She needed to get the plane into a steep ascent immediately. But she also knew that if she pulled too hard, the plane could stall and drop and they would plummet directly back into the ground.

By now everyone was plastered to the back of their seats as the plane shot skyward. All Emily could see was blue sky. The boulders and pine trees in front of them were out of sight. But the one thing she kept in her sights as the plane had been barreling down the runway was that one tall pine tree among the boulder outcrop directly in front of them. While soaring up, she tried disparately to keep the plane on the direct path toward the tree. Keeping the nose aimed directly at the top of the tree and in this steep ascent, she felt she had a chance the propellers would miss the tree. The plane under-belly would hit it. *One more nightmare if the propellers got caught in the tree. The plane in all likelihood would tip sideways and be hurtled to the ground.*

"Get the wheels up," she screamed at Peggy.

Peggy hit the landing gear lever just before they heard a loud "kaa . . .runch" and then "thump, thump, thump". The red warning light came on telling them the wheel wells did not close properly. Emily realized they had hit the top of the tree, but the plane was still holding steady, so they were safe. She reduced the speed and the ascent rate. Even with the warning light flashing and the incessant thumping, the plane kept flying. She was able to level out even more and finally able to see the ground ahead of them. They had passed the boulders and were headed for the mountains in the distance.

"What the hell just happened?" shouted Agent Daniels.

Thump, thump, thump.

"My plane," cried Carl.

Thump, thump, thump.

"Should we be worried?" Janice asked in a quivering voice.

"You took the top of the tree off and it's stuck in the wheel well, for god sake!" Peggy shouted. Emily finally had a chance to sneak a peek at Peggy. Her eyes were big as saucers, not to mention the sheer panic on her face.

Peggy reached over to re-open the wheel wells, but Emily grabbed her arm. "Don't do that. Opening the wells right now may slow us down and stall the plane. We only have 30 minutes flying time. Hopefully, when we open the wells to land, the tree branch will fall out."

"Are you kidding me? What if the wheels don't go down for our landing or worse yet, what if they're damaged when we land? With the landing speed, a broken wheel would mean we would lose control of the plane. It could spin around and break up into pieces!" Peggy wasn't speaking in a normal voice anymore. She was shouting at Emily.

Emily did not even respond. She checked the GPS. Using the yoke and rudder pedals, she flew slightly to the west, and entered the valley they planned to follow up to Missoula. She then straightened the plane out to continue on in a NNE direction. She took in a deep breath filling her lungs and blew it out in one quick breath. "Well, that's that. The worst is over. We'll worry about the wheels when we land " She looked over at Peggy and gave a weak smile. "One crisis at a time, Kiddo."

"I think we need to contact the Missoula Airport and tell them to prepare for an emergency landing," Peggy said.

"You're right. I'll contact them now," Emily said.

"Screw that, Emily. You just keep flying this plane. I'll do the contacting," Peggy said as she adjusted her headset. "Missoula Control, this is Cessna 14590. We are requesting preparations for an emergency landing. Over."

"Cessna 14590, we have already been instructed to institute those procedures by the National Air Traffic Control Center."

"I forgot," Emily said. "Tell them we'll need an ambulance standing by for Carl."

"Good idea." Peggy added the ambulance request to the Control Tower, but she did not tell the traffic controller the reason for the ambulance other than one of the passengers was hurt.

CHAPTER 28

• • •

EMILY TURNED HER HEAD AND looked at Peggy, but her calmness changed to pure terror when she looked out Peggy's window and saw a military jet flying close to their right wing. "Oh shit!" Emily yelled right before she put the plane into a tight left turn. She simultaneously used the foot pedals to work the rudder on the tail of the plane while she used the yoke to adjust the ailerons. Everything her flight instructor told her about banking whizzed through her memory. She checked the right side to see if the jet was still on their wing. It wasn't.

Peggy had only a nano-second to glimpse the jet before their plane banked. It looked huge! "Where did that jet come from?" Ever since they took off, she couldn't stop shouting. "Oh, this is just great. Now we're on a flight path to Spokane, for crying out loud.

A voice on their frequency came through their headsets. "Ladies, this is Lieutenant Commander Kevin Freeland from the Malmstrom Air Force Base. I'm here to escort your plane into the

Missoula Airport. Please turn the plane back to your original flight path."

"Oh really? And how am I supposed to do that with you right next to me?" Emily asked as she continued to fly west with the tall mountains looming in the distance. "If you want us back on our flight path, you just better move over so I can make my turn."

The military jet eased over to the right, but still kept the twin-engine off its left wing. "Okay. You can make your right turn now," the Lieutenant said. Slowly, Emily put their plane back on their flight path to Missoula.

"Ma'am, are you aware there is a tree branch stuck in your front wheel well and is that duct tape on the window?"

Emily kept her eyes front checking the instrument panel and the conditions in front of them. Flying with a jet so near them was unnerving. "Yes, to both questions. As to the branch well . . . I had to make a steep ascent on takeoff, because the runway was too short. I seemed to have hit the top of a tree on takeoff. The duct tape is there because the bad guys shot at our plane right before takeoff. We needed to keep the inside air pressure stable. Duct tape was all we had."

"Please repeat. You were shot at?"

"Yes."

"Is Vice President Andersen on board your airplane?" the pilot asked.

"Yes. He's sitting in the back," Peggy answered.

"I need to see him, Ma'am."

Peggy turned in her seat and spoke in a loud voice over the roar of the engines. "Bill, the jet pilot needs to see you to be sure you're on the plane. Put your face next to the window and wave at him."

Once Bill had his face next to the window, Peggy asked the jet pilot, "Do you see him back there?" He's at the third window in the back."

Actually, Bill saluted the pilot. No way was he going to be waving like some five year old kid.

"I need to speak to the Vice President, Ma'am. Have him come to the front and give him your headset."

After a few moments, Bill and Peggy made the co-pilot seat exchange and Bill put on the headset. Because the duct tape flower blossomed right in the middle of the window he had to scrunch down in the seat in order to look out of a tiny corner portion to see the pilot.

"Mr. Vice President, I'm Lieutenant Commander Kevin Freeland. Are you okay, Sir? Your pilot said your plane was shot at?"

Bill groaned silently. Bill did not want to broadcast any more information than was necessary over the open-air waves. Anything they said now could jeopardize nailing Patrick Webber later. "Yes, we were. Fortunately, no one was hurt. Sorry about this duct tape," he said hunched over trying to see the Air Force pilot. "What is our estimated time to Missoula, Lieutenant Commander?" Bill couldn't wait to get out of this plane. He didn't want to show fear during the ordeal. After all he was the Vice President of the United States. But truth be told, the take-off was sheer terror for him.

"Your ETA is 21 minutes, Sir."

"Thank you for your help. Now I'm going to turn things back over to Peggy, our co-pilot, so these ladies can fly the plane." Bill saluted the jet pilot as best he could out of the tiny portion at the bottom of the window. The pilot returned the salute.

CHAPTER 29

• • •

"THIS IS NBC NEWS IN New York. We interrupt our programming to bring you late breaking news. We have unconfirmed reports that Vice President, Bill Andersen, is making an unscheduled landing on board a private aircraft being flown into the Missoula, Montana Airport. He is not coming in on the official Air Force II that normally carries the Vice President. We will now switch to our NBC affiliate station in Missoula, Montana. Stacey Bole is standing by with a crew on the ground. Stacey what do we know so far regarding the Vice President?"

"Thank you, John. Since our cameras are not allowed on the Airport grounds at this moment, we are here on the parameter of the Missoula Airport. We have had reports that the Vice President is landing at this airport at any moment in a private aircraft. All takeoffs and landings have been suspended here awaiting the arrival of the Vice President. As you can see our camera is facing into the expected direction of the in-coming plane. As yet, the plane has not appeared. However, the sky above the Airport is completely empty of any in coming planes. We understand this is standard procedure when the President or Vice President fly into any airport in the country."

"Stacey, can you tell us why the Vice President is not flying in on the official Air Force II? How did he get on a private air craft?"

"I'm sorry, John. We have not been able to confirm the reason for the switch in aircraft. We will have that information to you as soon as it becomes available. To repeat, at the present time, our crew is being kept off the Airport grounds."

"Excuse me John. We have just received an unconfirmed report that the Vice President has been shot. We are working to confirm that."

"This is John Hudson in New York. As you just heard, NBC News has just received an unconfirmed report from our affiliate in Missoula, Montana that Vice President, Bill Andersen, has been shot. We now go to Edward Peck, the head of our NBC Washington Bureau. Edward, can you tell us if you have heard anything regarding the status of the Vice President Andersen?"

"No, John. The White House is being completely quiet on the condition of the Vice President. However, less than one hour ago, I and my colleagues did see a swarm of Secret Service Agents enter the Capitol Building. It was reported they entered the offices of the Speaker of the House and the President pro-tempore of the Senate.

That may mean if the Vice President isn't able to take over the duties of the Presidency, the line of succession goes to the Speaker of the House, to the President pro-Tempore of the Senate, or down to the Secretary of State."

"We now return to Stacy Bole standing by at our NBC Affiliate in Missoula, Montana."

"Thank you John. There are new developments here. We are swinging our camera over to the grounds of the Airport. Moments ago an ambulance and several fire trucks pulled up along the side of the runway. As you can see the firemen are now spreading a layer of form over the runway. We assume the Vice President's plane is expected to make an emergency landing. In the distance we can see a number of squad cars from the various local law enforcement departments entering the area and are approaching the runway. Around the corner of the main building, three black SUV's seem to be racing this way also. These could possibly be carrying members of the F.B.I. or Secret Service. Swinging our camera around to the direction of the expected flight path now, as of yet there is no sign of the plane with the Vice President aboard."

CHAPTER 30

• • •

AFTER THE VICE PRESIDENT RETURNED to his seat, Peggy began checking the controls. "You sure you don't want to let the wheels down and try to get rid of that tree branch?" she asked Emily.

"Not yet. We don't have that long before we start our descent. I'll do it then."

"Ladies," came the voice of the Lieutenant Commander. "Before you start your descent, I'm going to fly under your plane to check the tree branch and to see if there is any structural damage. Keep your plane steady at your current altitude and do not decrease your air speed."

"Oh, brother," mumbled Peggy.

Emily's hands tightened on the yoke. "Oh boy. This is a first," she said. Her eyes locked onto the instrument panel. She had to make sure the plane remained at the correct elevation and speed. "What an adventure this is, Peggy. Never in my life did I think we would be doing this. Have we got a story to tell our friends at our next flying club meeting."

Peggy did not take her eyes off the instrument panel either. She held her hands open on her lap in case she had to take control of the plane if needed. "I can't believe we got ourselves into this situation, Emily."

"Now hold your plane steady," said the Lieutenant Commander. With that he lowered his plane and flew underneath the twin engine. The clear top covering of his jet allowed him to view the underside of the twin engine above him. He started toward the nose to examine the wheel well that had a grip on the tree limb. The women were holding their plane nice and steady. He was able to slowly ease up on his speed and examined the rest of the under body of the plane. He couldn't believe those two old ladies had managed to fly the plane so perfectly over the top of the tree so that the propellers never touched a branch.

He slowed down even further until he was behind and out from under their plane, then he flew to the right and aligned his jet with their wing. "Other than the tree branch stuck in your front wheel well, I didn't see any other structural damage to the underside of your plane. Very nice flying, ladies." There was admiration in his voice.

"Thank goodness for that," Peggy said.

A smile broke out on Emily's face. She breathed calmly now. She couldn't remember if she took one breath of air during the entire time he was under their plane. "Thank you," she said over the radio. "Too bad your name isn't Roger. Then I could say 'Roger, Roger'."

With the good news, Peggy relaxed a bit and looked out her window at the jet pilot. "You know we can't see his face because his helmet has that tinted face shield," she said to Emily. "I bet he's a real cutie." She immediately heard a number of snickers in her headset.

"Ladies, you are on an open frequency. Please keep your communications on a professional level," the Lieutenant Commander ordered.

Peggy's brow furrowed and she grimaced in embarrassment. "You mean our conversation is being broadcast beyond just our two planes?" she asked.

"All the way to Washington, D.C., ma'am. Now why don't you open your wheel doors and dislodge the branch?"

Peggy sighed and turned to Emily. "See, I told you to do that."

Emily checked the distance to Missoula and their ETA to touch down. "We're going to begin our descent in five minutes. That will be the first thing we do, just not yet. I can't be sure lowering the wheels won't slow the plane down."

Actually, the two women were doing a good job of flying their plane. With all that went on, they didn't seem to be in a panic mode, the Lieutenant Commander thought. "Okay, I will be following you all the way to the runway," the pilot said. "If you choose to keep wheels up until your approach, you can. I'll keep an eye on the condition of your wheels as soon as you open the wells. Have you ever practiced an aborted landing?"

"We've done that a number of times in our training," Emily answered.

"How about an emergency landing? As we just heard from the Control Tower, foam is being spread on the runway right now. If your front wheel doesn't come down, you may have to pull the main landing gear up and land on the body of the plane or land on the two main wheels with the nose up. Think you can do that?" he asked.

Emily groaned. It was nerve-racking enough just flying the plane with the Vice President aboard without adding negative thoughts into the mix. She refused to think in those terms. She was the type of person who didn't waste energy dwelling on the what ifs of life. She studied and planned and then if something went wrong, she dealt with it then. She wasn't about to make herself lose her concentration about an imaginary emergency landing. "Listen, we are going to make it and everything will be fine, all right?" she barked.

Peggy groaned too, because she was the more pessimistic of the two. She always prepared for the worst and then was pleasantly surprised when things turned out okay. "Emily, promise me the first thing you'll do is lower the damn wheels the minute we start our descent."

"Of course. That's just what I'm planning to do."

After a few moments, the Missoula Control Tower broke into their conversation to inform them they could begin their descent. Because of the almost constant winds sweeping down from Canada, Missoula had only one long runway running from NNW to SSE. There were no planes airborne at the present time, since all had been diverted away from the Airport.

Emily adjusted the direction of the plane on a more northerly path, so she could bank shortly before the approach and come in on the northwest to southeast trajectory. She told the Lieutenant Commander she was going to open the wheels wells on three. He raised his jet above their wings. If the tree branch flew out of the wheel well in his direction and even nicked his plane, at these speeds major damage would be done to his aircraft.

While keeping her eyes on the instrument panel, she adjusted the wing flaps to reduce the airspeed. She grabbed Peggy's arm for a moment. "Here goes nothing, kiddo. Get ready." Peggy gave her friend's hand a return squeeze.

"Three, two, one."

Peggy reached over and lowered the landing gear lever.

At first nothing happened. Terror started creeping into their souls.

Now. . . Emily started to review the emergency landing procedures in her mind.

Peggy went into her usual panic mode and uttered, "Oh, God." But then before she could panic further, they heard a beautiful *thunk* as the doors opened and the wheels came down. They felt the plane start to slow down. It was the normal slow down they always felt when the wheels were lowered.

"It worked! The branch is out!" Peggy shouted as she raised her fists in the air. "Woohoo!" But then she looked at the instrument panel and re-panicked. Only the two side wheel lights had turned green. "The green light on the front wheel well isn't on," she shouted.

"Roger!" Emily shouted to the Air Force pilot. She was so terrified, she forgot his name and called him 'Roger'. "Check to see if all three wheels are free,"

When the lieutenant heard Peggy panic about the light not on, he had immediately flown down to examine the front wheel. It was down and looked to be in landing position. "I've already dropped down and examined the underside of your plane, Ma'am. I can see all three wheels out. There doesn't appear to be any structural damage to the front wheel. "However, you still have time to abort the landing, if you chose," the Lieutenant answered her as calmly as he could.

"And then what? We just keep flying around." Emily asked in exasperation. "Chances are we'll run out of gas doing that. No, aborting isn't the answer. We have to go in nose up."

He flew lower an examined the front wheel one more time. "As I said, there doesn't look to be any structural damage. The front wheel is down and looks to be in the correct landing position. The green light may not be on because of electrical rather than structural damage.

"That's it then. We're going in for a landing with the nose up for as long as we can," Emily said.

• • •

Stacy Bole of the Montana T. V. news continued her nonstop reporting. "We have been watching the fireman finishing up spreading a layer of foam on the runway. They are definitely preparing for a crash landing of the Vice President's plane. Wait a minute. We have just received word that his plane has begun its decent. We'll swing our camera around in the direction of the expected landing. There, we can now see the Vice President's plane off in the distance as it comes in for a landing here at the Missoula Airport. It appears an Air Force jet is flying alongside of his plane escorting it to the airfield."

"Stacey, something just fell out of the Vice President's plane. Can you tell what it was?" the New York newsperson asked.

"No, John, from this distance we can't tell what was just jettisoned out of the plane. It appears to be some sort of long narrow object."

"Do you know what it was that fell from the plane, Stacey?"

"It's hard to tell, John. But something definitely came out of the bottom of the plane. As you can see, the Air Force jet dipped slightly after the object fell out of the Vice President's plane. We don't know if the pilot was trying to examine exactly what it was."

"We go to our Washington correspondent. Edward. Has the White House issued any statement on the condition of the Vice President or who is flying his plane? Are you getting a live feed where you are? Something has just been jettisoned out of his plane. With the distance from the Airport, our camera could not pick up exactly what the object was. Is there anything coming from the White House yet?"

"No, John. The White House has been completely silent. No one is saying a word as of yet. However, here in the Press Room other reports from the major networks with affiliates in Missoula have reported seeing the object fall also. All reports state the Vice President's plane was too far away to state exactly what the object was. Hold on, John. Reports are coming in that it could have been part of the plane that may account for the foaming on the runway. Another report states that the object could have been some sort of high powered weapon given the fact of the Air Force jet escort. With the reports of the Vice President being shot, this seems like a likely scenario."

CHAPTER 31

• • •

THE LIEUTENANT COMMANDER DID NOT want to spoil the women's optimism, but this could turn into a very dangerous situation if the front wheel was damaged in any way. The life and safety of the Vice President was at stake. He had to bring them out of their euphoria and quickly. "However, I would, also, advise you to prepare for a nose up landing. Once you land try to keep the nose up as long as you can before you put the plane's weight on the front wheel. If you do that, by then your speed will have been reduced and this will minimize any unforeseen problems. "

Peggy slumped in her seat. "Oh no."

"Knock it off, Peggy" Emily snapped. The airport was in sight and she didn't have time to deal with her friend's negativity. "He gave us good advice. All planes land with the nose up, so no sweat there. It's going to be keeping it up as long as we can. That's going to be a first for us. I need you to concentrate on the landing, so get yourself together right now and help me."

Peggy responded to Emily's remarks and got control of herself. She began to call out the altitude as the Airport loomed before them.

The plane was now down to 4,000 feet above the ground. Emily banked the plane to line up with the runway. Once the plane straightened out, she decreased the speed and then ever so slightly pulled back on the yoke and brought the nose up while she lowered the wing flaps decreasing the speed and altitude even more. Emily held the nose up as the plane dropped to 3,000, 2,000, 1,000 feet. The air speed decreased accordingly. She wanted to land at the minimum speed.

Neither of them could believe the amount of fire trucks and cars they saw lined up along the runway. They could see the white foam covering it. Their blood pressure went up until they got closer and realized they could still see the runway markers through the foam. They had to be very sure they could see where to set the plane down upon landing.

"You're doing a good job, ladies. The nose is up right where it should be." The Air Force pilot was impressed with how they were handling the plane.

Emily tried to slow the plane down as much as she could without putting the plane into a stall. That's all they needed right now. 500, 400, 300 feet to touchdown. She and Peggy had to use all their skills on this – reduce speed and keep plane wings even with the horizon using ailerons, nose up using yoke, keep tail rudder steady using foot pedals, cut engines at correct time so plane would *coast* but not stall. The Control Tower began calling the altitude -- 100, 50, 25 feet.

"The moment of truth," Emily whispered to herself as she pushed the yoke ever so slightly. The plane skimmed over the No Landing Zone. The side wheels touched down onto the runway. "Nose up, nose up, nose up," Emily kept repeating to herself like a mantra. Finally, when the speed was down as much as possible, she brought the nose down and the front wheel gently made contact with the ground and held. The plane continued to slow down. The front wheel had not been damaged. It came to a complete stop near the end of the runway.

"Saaa-weet!" they heard the Air Force pilot say as his jet zoomed passed their plane on the right side. He then revved his engines and made a rapid ascent. "Beautiful flying, ladies!" Peggy and Emily watched as he toggled his wings at them before flying off.

The women shut the plane down and sat there grinning at each other. They did a "high-five". Cheers went up behind them as the four passengers unbuckled their seat belts. Everyone seemed to be talking at once.

"Never a doubt," Janice said although her face was still drained of all color.

"Never thought my plane would survive," Carl said still in his seat.

The emergency people outside were knocking on the door. Secret Service Agent Daniels did not open the side door instead he came to the front of the plane. "Now listen up, people," he announced. "None of you." He looked over at the three women and stared at them. "And, I mean none of you can say a word about what went on at Burnt Fork Lake. The Vice President has briefed me about what happened during the past several days. There will be a thorough investigation into Patrick Webber and those who were involved in the kidnapping plot. It is imperative that you do not jeopardize the investigation by giving any press interviews. All press releases will come from the White House." Again he looked at the women. "Is that understood? Not one word even to your family or friends."

The three women's shoulders sagged. Their faces were void of all expression. After all they had done for the Vice President, the three women felt hurt by the way the Agent was treating them. They had put their lives in danger for Bill, and his Agent was accusing them of not having a brain in their heads. Of course, they knew not to talk about what happened.

Bill quickly walked to the front. "Go sit down," he told his Agent. He turned to the women. "For the rest of my life, I will never be able to thank you enough for what you did for me. The three of you went way beyond the call of duty. A thank you seems so inadequate." Bill's word made the women feel better. He turned his body so he included Carl in the conversation. "My Agent was abrupt speaking to you, but you have to understand, there will be an investigation into what happened. We can't let people like Patrick Webber get away with this. Not just you, but all of us has to monitor what we say in public. One misstep and his attorneys will pounce on it and twist our words. You know it and I know it. Now we're going to have to let the people outside into the plane. I probably won't be able to speak with you when they come. Just know you are all leaving huge footprints in my life and I will never forget what you did for me."

He started to shake Janice's hand then he just grabbed her and gave her a bear hug. Tears welled up in his eyes. Peggy held out her arms. "Thank you," he said. By now tears were streaming down Emily's face when he opened his arms to her.

"By the way, Peggy and I only got our twin-engine pilot's license 30 days ago, I thought you should know," she whispered in his ear.

Bill broke out in a strangled sob and laugh at the same time. He didn't have time to question her more, because the pounding on the door became more frantic. Agent Daniels had to let everyone in.

A team of FBI agents entered and stood beside the Vice President. The EMTs entered next. Agent Daniels directed them to Carl. Bill would not let them take him off the plane until Carl was taken care of first. Carl tried to stand and told them he could walk out of the plane, but the three women like mother hens protested and demanded he stay seated and be carried out on a stretcher. Because the plane was so narrow, the EMTs had to bring a flat board in. Carl was lowered onto the board and the men carried him down the steps and set him on a waiting stretcher.

Next Agent Daniels and the FBI escorted Bill from the plane. One FBI agent stayed behind. "Come with me ladies. The Vice President has to do a short press conference in the terminal and would like you to be present. There is a van waiting to take you there.

"What about Carl's plane. We just can't leave it here," Emily said.

"Arrangements have been made to get it off the runway and into a hanger, Ma'am," he answered.

• • •

The T.V. cameras stayed zeroed in on the plane coming in. "As you can see, John, the Vice President's plane is now coming in for a landing. It has now touched down. Are you able to see the strange marking on the pilot's window? I would say it looks like duct tape. The plane has now stopped at the end of the runway and is sitting there. It doesn't appear to be making any attempt to taxi to the terminal. The law enforcement people are pounding on the plane door, but it is not being opened. There doesn't seem to be any response inside the plane. At this point, we don't know if the Vice President is alive or he is being held captive."

"Okay, the door has just been opened. The stairs are being lowered. Men in suits, we presume them to be FBI agents are storming into the plane now. The EMTs with various first-aid equipment are following them into the plane. The local law enforcement teams have surrounded the Vice President's plane. As yet, no one is leaving the plane, however, one of the EMTs has just approached the door and requested a board be handed up to him. Again all remains quiet in the plane."

"The EMTs are carefully coming out now. They have a body on the board. We can't tell if it is Vice President Bill Andersen, because, the person's head is covered in a multi-colored bandage. We've never seen a bandage like this. The ends are hanging down the sides of the person's head. There is a large white cloth wrapped around the person's shoulder and arm. It appears to be some sort of sling. Again, because of all the strange bandages, we are unable to tell if the person is the Vice President. However, the ambulance is leaving the area with red lights flashing. You can see it speeding to the exit."

"No wait a minute. Vice President Andersen is exiting the plane right now! He appears to be unharmed. He is coming down the steps surrounded by FBI agents who entered the plane moments ago. He now is being escorted to the waiting black SUV. Another FBI agent is now leaving the plane. He is being followed down the steps by three older women. We have no idea who these women are or what they were doing on the Vice President's plane."

CHAPTER 32

• • •

NANCY WAS SITTING IN A Strategic Planning meeting with the company CEO and six other executive vice presidents when her cell phone vibrated and went off, vibrated again and went off. On the third vibration she couldn't stand it anymore. She looked at phone and saw she had received two phone calls and a text message. She surreptitiously held the phone below the table to check her text message. It was from Amy. Without opening the full text, she was able to read the top few words of the text: EMERGENCY. MOTHERS. She fought for control as she tried to process those words. Her fingers were shaking as she opened the full text: EMERGENCY. MOTHERS. Call me IMMEDIATELY!!!! She stood up and excused herself and walked to the back of the room. She pressed "A" on her speed dial.

Amy answered on the first ring. "Do you have access to a T.V.? Never in a thousand years will you believe where our mothers are."

"Has something happened to them? Oh god, Amy. I just knew something would happen. Are they all right?"

"They're fine. But get to a T.V. as fast as you can. You won't believe what they're involved in now."

"What channel?" Nancy asked. By this time, not only were her fingers shaking, her entire body was quivering.

"Pick one. They're on all the major networks. Oh, Nancy, you won't believe this. Hurry up. Hurry up. Get to a T.V and then call me back." With that Amy disconnected the phone call.

For a brief moment Nancy just stood there trying to grasp the meaning of Amy's bizarre phone call. Then she did something that was so out of character of her cool, contained, *I am in control self*. She shouted! "I've got to find a television! Something has happened to my mother!" With that, she ran out of the room and left the CEO and six executives seated at the table with their mouths open and eyes wide in shock.

She raced to one of the other presentation rooms on the floor. She knew it had a television. She threw open the door of the room stunning the employees who were there for their meeting.

"I'm sorry, but I need to use the T.V.," she announced. She paid no further attention to the people as she grabbed the remote control and turned it on. The Montana NBC channel came on just as she saw her mother and Peggy and Janice getting into a black SUV. It was parked on an airport runway. *What the heck is going on?* She had no idea where her mother was. The NBC announcer in New York was speaking. "While we are waiting for the Vice President to speak to the press in the Missoula Airport, we are rerunning the tape of his arrival on a private twin-engine plane."

By this time the top executives had regained their composure and were flooding into the meeting room to see what was happening. The employees in the room were further stunned to see the top echelon of the company barrel in behind Nancy.

What does our mothers have to do with the Vice President? Nancy pushed Amy's phone number.

Again Amy answered on the first ring. "What channel are you watching? I'll synchronize with you."

"NBC. Amy, for heaven's sake, what is going on?" Nancy demanded.

"Okay, see that plane coming in with the Air Force jet following it. Nancy, our mothers were on that plane!!!"

"What?" was the only word Nancy was able to utter as she watched the plane approaching. The announcer had just said their technical crew had reviewed the original tape recording and were able to determine it was a tree branch that had fallen out of the plane's front wheel well. She sat there with her hand over her mouth and watched as the branch fell and the plane came in for a landing. By this time everyone in the room was crowded around the television watching the patched-up plane come in for a landing. She heard the announcer say something about duct tape.

What's going on, Nancy?" the CEO asked her.

"I have no idea," she mumbled. "My friend," she held her cell phone away from her ear and pointed it toward her boss without taking her eyes off the T.V. "told me our mothers were on that plane."

The door to the plane had been opened and she saw a man being lowered onto a stretcher. After that the Vice President emerged.

"Wait for it. Wait for it," Amy's voice came over the phone. "Now – there they come. Can you believe it, Nancy? It's our mothers!"

"Oh my god, you're right," Nancy said. "How did they get on that plane?"

"I have no idea," Amy answered.

"*The Vice President is now in place to make a short statement,*" said the NBC announcer.

The people around Nancy were talking. She turned up the volume and watched as Bill Andersen came to the podium. Camera flashes were going off like crazy. And there in the background stood the three women. They looked very serious and scared. They were disheveled. Their clothes were wrinkled and dirty. Their hair wasn't combed. None of them had on any make-up, which gave them an even more washed out pallor.

"I will be making a brief statement" the Vice President began. "However, I won't be taking any questions. The White House will be holding a press conference later today and be issuing a formal statement at that time."

"I was on a short R & R vacation in western Montana earlier this week. I did not fly aboard the official Air Force II, since the runway that services the cabin where I stayed was man-made and could not support an Air Force II landing. Therefore, I flew to Montana in a private jet accompanied by my Secret Service detail. The jet I flew in on and another twin-engine plane both landed on the same runway. While there, our jet developed mechanical trouble and could not take off. Unfortunately, the pilot of the twin-engine plane was injured which made it impossible for him to fly his plane out of the camping area. He was the gentleman who was taken off our plane on a stretcher. However," Bill motioned for Emily and Peggy to step forward, "since I had to be back in Washington, D.C., these two ladies who are licensed pilots were able to fly us all out in the twin-engine plane."

"Aren't those women a little too old to be flying a plane?" A reporter's comment was heard from the back of the room.

Janice immediately stomped forward to join her friends. Everyone in the room and those watching the live broadcast saw three jaws clamp shut; six pairs of eyes become tiny slits; and, three lips purse tightly as the women glared at the reporter.

After all his years in politics, Bill had trained himself never to show any reaction to any reporter's question or comment no matter how dumb it was. Internally, he wanted to throw his hands up in disgust, roll his eyes and shout, "Son of a bitch" for that reporter's stupid remark. He remained calm and did none of those things, but before he could mollify the three women, Emily blurted out," You got a problem with that, Cupcake?" Peggy and Janice nodded their heads in agreement. They looked like dashboard doll ornaments in a '57 Chevy. Their heads were bobbing up and down so fast. Out of the corner of his eye he saw the furious expression on Agent Daniel's face.

He needed to get control of the situation and right now before the three female commandos started World War III. "The women did a fine job of piloting the plane," he added hastily. "We flew into the Missoula Airport since the runway here can sustain a large jet landing. I will be flying back to Washington D. C. shortly on a military plane out of Malmstrom Air Force Base. I don't have any additional comments to make at this time, but again, the White House will be holding a press conference later today. I'm sure you will have a chance to have your questions answered at that time. Thank you." With that he turned and walked off the podium and was immediately surrounded by Agent Daniels and several FBI agents. However, that didn't stop the reporters. They continued to shout out questions as he left the podium.

"Did the President know you were in Montana?"

"Who shot at your plane?"

"What fell out of your plane as you were landing?"

The FBI Agent who had given the women a ride to the terminal quickly approached them. "Come with me . . . now," he ordered in sotto voce. The authority in his voice made the women follow along as he exited the stage.

"Can you imagine being called too old to be flying? What an airhead to say something like that," Peggy said.

"Wait until they find out what else we did at Burnt Fork Lake. They won't be talking to us like that anymore," Emily said in a snit.

The FBI agent stopped, turned and looked directly at each of them. "Ladies . . . shut up."

They stopped in their tracks and assumed a haughty stance. "Hey," Emily said. The agent grabbed her arm and began to march her down the hall. Peggy and Janice had to really scurry to keep up with the two. Once they were out of the terminal, he escorted them to the SUV parked at the curb and drove off.

The network cameras followed the Vice President and his entourage through the terminal. Since they were not allowed beyond the building onto the tarmac, when Bill exited and walked out on the runway, they lined up at the inside windows and filmed him getting on a military transport plane that had landed while he was giving his news conference. As soon as the Vice President was on board, the huge plane taxied to the end of a runway and took off turning east. None of the cameras bothered filming the whereabouts of the three women.

• • •

Nancy was in a daze. It took her a moment to react to her surroundings again. When she did, she realized her co-workers were cheering. When her mother had said, 'You got a problem with that, Cupcake', she heard someone shout, "Way to go." She looked around the room. These people weren't making fun of her mother. They were cheering for her. *Why haven't I understood that before?*

" Wow, Nancy. Your mother actually flew the plane for the Vice President."

"I don't think my mother could do that."

"How fantastic is that?"

"Nancy, your mother is awesome!"

She put her elbow on the table and cupped her chin in her hand. There was a smile on her face. "Yeah, my mother is awesome," she said quietly.

Somewhere along the line she had set her phone down on the table. She picked it up. "Amy, are you still there?"

"Yes. Nancy, I just can't believe what these three have done. Can you?"

"Listen, Amy, we've got to call them and find out what actually happened. The Vice President sure sounded cryptic, didn't he? I know there is more to this."

The two daughters hung up. Nancy immediately called her mother's cell phone. It kept ringing and went to voice mail. She groaned.

CHAPTER 33

• • •

As the Vice President's plane landed in Missoula two military helicopters were one hour out from landing at Burnt Fork Lake. One carried a six-man Navy Seal team with two additional medics, and the other helicopter carried a team of ten FBI agents who would gather all the forensic evidence once the area was secured. When Bill called the White House using the extreme danger code, the computer zeroed in on his exact location. It then scanned the surrounding area locating the cabins, the sheds and the airstrip. After Bill got on board the twin-engine plane, he also informed Washington about the location of Patrick Webber and his hired goon and the location of all the known weapons. He reported how Janice saw his Agent and the other man drop their weapons before going back into the woods. Therefore, the Seals did not think stealth would be necessary. It was determined the two helicopters could land directly on the airstrip and the team would fan out from there.

After landing, a team headed in the direction of Peggy's shed where Webber and another man were reported to being held. Another team headed in the direction where the Secret Service Agent and the other man had been reported shot. Before the third team headed for Patrick Webber's cabin, they boarded Webber's jet and freed the two pilots who vehemently denied any involvement in the Vice President's kidnapping. The Team brought the pilots back and handcuffed them to a bench and shackled their legs to the floor on the side of the first helicopter. This team had orders to then check both Webber's cabin and shed where the Vice President was reportedly held.

Once on the ground all the Seals proceeded to their assigned areas with the usual extreme caution however. They moved quietly from cover to cover using boulders and trees, then scanned the area ahead before moving forward, making sure they also covered their partner as they moved. At the beginning of the tree line surrounding the airfield, the team searching for the two men who had been shot located and collected the three guns dropped by the Bill's Secret Service Agent and the other unidentified man. They secured the guns in an evidence box the FBI had provided. They picked up the blood trails of the two men. As they were tracking them, they received a call from the Team who were now at Webber's cabin. Both the Agent and the other wounded man were found in the cabin and needed medical attention, they were told. They hurried to the cabin. Both of the wounded men had been lucky to get to the cabin. As the Seal team were on their way, they could hear sounds of several cougars roaming in the area. Apparently the animals had smelled the blood and were closing in. The Seals treated the threat of an attack by the cougars as they would any other enemy threat and walked with their weapons ready to fire.

When the team arrived at Webber's cabin, they found the Agent barely conscious. The other man said his name was "John Smith" and he had no knowledge of the Vice President being kidnapped. The medic immediately started an I.V. and checked the bullet wounds of the Agent. He used a tourniquet to stem the flow of blood to his leg and foot. He then added pain medication to the I.V. The Agent slowly responded to the I.V. He was still weak but now conscious. He told the Seals he was not involved in the kidnapping of the Vice President. He said he was shot by one of Webber's men as he was trying to defend the Vice President.

Three of the four Navy Seals and the medic were able to carry the Secret Service Agent and walk the other man back to the copter. One Seal remained at the cabin. When they reached the helicopter, the Seals strapped and handcuffed the Agent on a stretcher and handcuffed and shackled "John Smith" to the bench. The medic stayed on board to tend to the two wounded men while the three Seals escorted the FBI team back to Webber's cabin so that they could begin their forensic investigations.

Before they left the helicopter, they handed over the box with the three guns they found on the ground. The FBI secured the evidence boxes with the guns to be checked for fingerprints later. At Webber's cabin the team contacted the team responsible for securing Peggy's cabin and shed to let them know they would be escorting four of the FBI agents to their site.

When the team broke the lock on Peggy's shed they found Patrick Webber and another man bound and laying on the shed floor. They were amazed at how intricate each man had been bound. One Seal immediately cut the rope around the canoe. Now they wouldn't have to worry about it falling on top of any of them as they untied Webber and the unidentified man. They cut the ropes holding the paddle behind Webber's back first. As soon as the tape was removed from Webber's mouth, he told the Seals he had been kidnapped along with the Vice President. He demanded to know if the Seals had found the Vice President, since he was bound and taken to another location. He told them his captors looked Middle-eastern, and he had no idea who the other man in the shed was.

Webber's hired man just glared at him but didn't say a word. He had been in trouble with the law before. He knew the drill. He would bide his time and make a deal when the time was right.

Once both men were freed, the Seals waited inside the shed for the FBI agents to arrive. Both the Navy Seals and the ten FBI agents had been briefed on what had really happened at Burnt Fork

Lake. They were aware it was Patrick Webber who was the alleged mastermind behind the kidnapping of the Vice President. They just stared at him as they brought their weapons up and waited.

When the FBI agents entered the shed, Patrick Webber was immediately handcuffed and put under arrest. He was read his rights. The FBI did not want to make any stupid mistakes that would allow Webber to get off on a technicality. He protested the entire time he was led back to the helicopter and demanded an attorney. He kept repeating that he too had been kidnapped. The two FBI agents who would be escorting him back to Washington D. C. did not secure Webber with the other prisoners. They led him to the second helicopter and kept him separate. Once Webber was on board, handcuffed and legs shackled to the floor, both helicopters took off. The eight FBI agents and the two of the Navy Seals would remain at Burnt Fork to gather forensic evidence.

At Malmstrom Air Force Base the prisoners were taken off the helicopters and transferred to a military cargo plane to be flown to Washington D.C. The plane would fly directly to Andrews Air Force Base where the prisoners would be taken into custody by Federal Marshalls.

CHAPTER 34

• • •

BECAUSE THE MAIN FBI HEADQUARTERS in Montana was located in Great Falls, Emily, Peggy and Janice were taken to a room in a Federal building in Missoula for a debriefing. All three women agreed before they would answer any questions about what happened at Burnt Fork Lake, they wanted to contact their families to let them know they were okay.

"You cannot tell your family members one thing about the Vice President being kidnapped or what role you played in his rescue. Is that understood?" Agent Krall said.

"We already know that, Agent Krall," Janice said. "Bill warned us not to say anything to anyone, because it could jeopardize the case against Patrick Webber. But, we still want to assure our families we're okay. They must be frantic by now."

"We'll need your phone to make our calls," Peggy said. "Our phones are out of juice and need to be recharged. But I have a problem." She looked at her two friends. "I don't know about you, but I don't know my son's phone number. With these cells phones I just press his name when I call him. I haven't dialed his phone number in years."

"Good grief. You're right, Peggy. The only way I know to get in touch with Amy is to press "A" on the call menu. Now what do we do?"

"Well, I think I could call Nancy's company and ask for her," Emily said. She looked at Agent Krall, "Could you look up the number on your computer for me?"

Agent Krall passed a pen and tablet to the women. "I can do better than that. Each of you write the name of the children you want to call and I'll get their cell phone numbers out of the FBI data base."

Janice wrote down Amy's name. "You can do that?" she asked. "Oh, my. We have no privacy left at all, do we?"

Within minutes, the three women had the phone numbers of their children and were able to make their calls.

When Amy asked her mother what was going on, Janice told her she couldn't talk about it right now. She told Amy to be sure to watch the press briefing at the White House.

"Oh Mom, only you would get involved in something clandestine like this," Amy chuckled. "Can you at least tell me where you are and that you're okay?"

"I'm fine, Honey, and I'm still in Missoula. I'll call you when I get home."

Peggy's call to her son was a little more somber because he had not been watching the news reports and had no idea his mother flew a plane with the Vice President on board. She had to reassure him she was fine without going into much detail. She too told him to watch the White House press briefing.

Emily's call to Nancy did not go smoothly. The minute Emily said hello, Nancy fired off a litany of questions.

"Where are you? How did you get on the plane with the Vice President? Did you actually pilot the plane? Why haven't you returned my phone calls? Do you know how worried I've been?"

Emily tried several times to interject answers, but Nancy, the executive control freak, didn't stop. Emily finally gave up and waited until Nancy ran out of steam. Then she told her she wasn't allowed to say what had happened, but she should watch the White House press briefing for more details. And that, of course, caused Nancy to go bezerk. Finally, Emily told her she and Peggy and Janice had to answer questions for the FBI and would call her when she got home.

The people at the table heard Nancy's scream just before Emily pushed the disconnect button. The FBI agent had a smile on his face as Emily gave the phone back to the him.

During the phone calls, a Federal Marshall stationed at the Missoula County Court House entered the room and took a seat next to Agent Krall. Along with taping the interview with the women, the FBI requested a Federal Marshall be present so the defense attorney could not challenge the authenticity of the interview. The women were also asked to sign a sworn statement attesting to the date, the time of the interview and that they gave their testimony willingly. The severity of this act of kidnapping the Vice President demanded that all "T's" were cross and all "I's" were dotted. No one wanted to see Patrick Webber get off, because someone screwed up.

"Now I am going to debrief the three of you. Our conversation will be recorded. I will direct my questions to each of you individually. If any of you have additional comments, raise your hand and I'll call on you. Please do not talk while someone else is speaking." Agent Krall turned on the recorded and looked at the clock on the wall.

"This is FBI Agent John Krall of the Great Falls, Montana FBI office. The time is 2:23 p.m. on Friday, October 18, 2015. I am interviewing Emily Jackson, Janice Winters and Margaret (Peggy) Cunes regarding the events at Burnt Fork Lake, Montana and the alleged kidnapping of William Andersen, the Vice President of the United States."

"Will each of you please state your name and address for the record? We will start with Emily Jackson."

"Now Emily can you state exactly when you and your friends arrived at the cabin in Burnt Fork Lake, Montana?"

And so the briefing began. The women told him of seeing the twin-engine plane land while they were hiking. All three testified they did not see the jet plane land but they did hear it flying overhead, and then heard the sound of it landing.

He asked them to explain in detail why they thought the Vice President was in trouble and who was in the entourage when they met him on the path. Where was the exact location when they met him? Where was each person standing? How did they know Webber had the last cabin?

He couldn't say anything on tape, but he made a mental note to congratulate the women for their courage when they rescued the Vice President and the wounded pilot from the shed. When he was assigned to escort the women from the plane and terminal today, he felt he had drawn the short straw. Now he was in awe of these women.

The most in-depth questions came when Janice had to describe how she and the Vice President met up with Patrick Webber. She was asked to recall the exact words that were spoken. When asked how she ended up with the gun, Janice decided not to tell him she took the gun from Bill because she thought Bill was going to shoot Webber. Those were her thoughts not actual fact, so she said she took the gun from the Vice President so he could subdue Webber.

Agent Krall learned Peggy hit one of Webber's men with a frying pan and then hit Webber with a shovel when he tried to run out of the shed. Again he asked for the exact words Webber said to them at the door of the shed about offering them money.

He was stunned when he heard them tell about being shot at and lowered his head as he tried to hide a smile when Peggy told him how they put duct tape over the bullet holes. He thought he had heard it all until Janice told him how she shot the Secret Service Agent and other man as they were firing their guns.

Both the FBI agent and the Federal Marshall smiled as Emily told him about getting the tree branch stuck in the wheel well.

"This interview is over at 4:52 p.m. Friday, October 18, 2015." Krall pushed the stop button on the recorder. He looked across the table at the three women and smiled. "You three were awesome. I hope the President gives you a medal for what you did. Do you realize because of your heroic actions, you were responsible for saving the life of the Vice President?" Even the Federal Marshall leaned across the table and shook their hands.

Because Agent Krall had been so reticent for most of the day, the three friends were stunned at his words. The enormity of what they had done hadn't sunk in yet. The women looked at each other and smiled sheepishly.

CHAPTER 35

• • •

WHEN THE VICE PRESIDENT ARRIVED at Andrews Air Force Base, he was met by a new detail of Secret Service Agents. They boarded helicopter, Marine II, which then flew directly to the White House lawn. From there he was escorted to the Situation Room in the basement of the White House for his debriefing The Secret Service detail did not allow him to speak with anyone along the way.

When they entered the Room, in addition to the top FBI Agent in charge of his debriefing, there were five attorneys and a court stenographer from the Department of Justice, the Attorney General, the Heads of the FBI, the CIA, and Homeland Security. The President and his Chief of Staff and the Chairman of the Joint Chiefs of Staff rounded out the participants at the table.

Before the FBI Agent started to record the debriefing, he said, "We all understand the severity of the events of the past few days. I will be leading this debriefing. I understand each of you represents an arm of our government that will be playing a crucial role in the outcome of these events. However, while this debriefing is going on, I am cautioning everyone in this room to remain silent. Do not interject additional questions into this particular interview. Write them down. Any questions you may have concerning your areas of expertise regarding the Montana events must wait until the debriefing is concluded. It is imperative the Vice President be allowed to fully concentrate on the events as they unfolded. Is this understood?" The people in the room nodded their agreement. One or two of them had a look of contempt on their faces, as if the lowly FBI Agent had the affront to tell them what to do.

The tape recorder was turned on and the debriefing was conducted in the same manner as the women's debriefing in Montana. Bill was asked to begin with the reason for the decision to accompany Patrick Webber to Montana was made. The questions followed a chronological time-line order. Along with the tape recording, the DOJ stenographer sat quietly along the wall and transcribed every word spoken by both the FBI Agent and the Vice President.

Again, the Agent's questions became very in-depth when Bill described meeting Webber on the forest path. The Agent wanted to know exactly what Webber said. Several times he asked Bill to repeat his answer.

Although Bill had kept his phone conversations with Washington hazy as to the role the three women had played, he now related all they had done for him in Montana – freeing Carl and him from the shed, Janice helping him secure Patrick Webber, how they got his Agent off Webber's jet, shooting the two men and how and why Emily and Peggy piloted the twin-engine plane. And same as Montana, several smiles broke out around the table regarding the branch stuck in the wheel well.

The people at the table dealt with plots against the United States on a daily basis. Globally they were inured by man's inhumanity to man. But even the most jaded of these members was appalled at Webber's sinister plot against the men who held the highest office in the United States. Some of those in the clandestine organizations thought of ways to have Patrick Webber quietly killed. Yet they all knew killing Webber wouldn't stop the plots. There would always be someone else stepping forward to fill his shoes.

When the debriefing was concluded, the President rose from his chair before any of the people could bombard Bill with their questions. "Ladies and gentlemen, the Vice President has been through a terrifying ordeal. He has had little if any sleep for the past twenty-four hours. Therefore, I am requesting you save any questions you might have until tomorrow. Bill needs to go home and be with his family. My Chief of Staff will work out a schedule for tomorrow and the next day allotting you private time to conduct your interviews with him."

Bill was exhausted. He gave a weak smile and mouthed a "thank you" to the President. No one at the table argued with the

President's request to hold their questions. All of them knew the future of keeping their appointed jobs rested in his hands. Like they were ordered, they would contact his Chief of Staff and make their appointments for an interview with the Vice President.

"Before we leave this room," the Attorney General said as she rose from her chair. "It is vital that none of you mentions to *anyone* the things you have heard here tonight. Above all do not talk to any politicians on the hill and especially to the press about what you have heard. That is the easiest way for leaks and innuendos to be past along. The press is in a feeding frenzy right now. Any tidbit they can get their hands on from anyone will be blown all out of proportion, and it will spread like wildfire. I want to stress this – none of us can jeopardize the case that will be brought against Patrick Webber."

The President and his Chief of Staff left the room first. They had to meet with the Attorney General and her staff to prepare a press briefing. Their overwhelming task would be to announce what had happened to Bill in Montana. The Department of Justice hadn't even had a chance to formally charge Patrick Webber in the D.C. courts yet. If he was charged by the time of the press briefing, his name could be mentioned.

The Secret Service Agents immediately surrounded Bill and whisked him out of the room. They knew once the President left the other people would swarm in and try to get his attention. He really looked exhausted now. He needed to see his family, and most of all he needed to sleep.

• • •

"Good evening, ladies and gentlemen," the President's Press Secretary began the press briefing two hours later. "I will be reading a prepared press release and will take a few of your questions."

"On Wednesday of this week Vice President, William Andersen, flew to western Montana on board a private jet owned by Patrick Webber. While in Montana the Vice President was held without his consent for approximately sixteen hours. He was subsequently freed unharmed and was then flown to the Missoula Airport. A military aircraft then flew him back to Washington, D. C. The military plane landed at Andrews Air Force Base at 4:45 p.m. this afternoon."

"Thirty minutes ago in the Washington D. C. Federal Court, the Attorney General, Amanda Prescott, brought charges of kidnapping against Patrick Webber in the unlawful detainment of the Vice President of the United States. In addition, similar charges were brought against Secret Service Agent, James Kovac, John Howard, and Brian Clemmons who were in the employ of Mr. Webber."

"The FBI in Montana is in the process of collecting forensic evidence around the camping area where the Vice President had been staying. Further charges against additional persons are expected to be filed within the next few days."

He was not allowed to mention Burnt Fork Lake as the exact location in Montana, since the FBI still had the area closed off while they continued their investigation. Mere mention of it would have the press and rubberneckers of the public swarming all over the crime scene.

"Now, I will take a few of your questions. However, in view of the severity of the charges and the early stages of the on-going investigation, I may not be able to provide answers tonight. But I want to stress, that President Mellon has requested there be daily press briefings held as new information regarding this tragic event comes to light."

It was the first time in Presidential press conference history that it began with every single correspondent's hand raised with a question. The Press Secretary was severely warned about inadvertently stating something that could jeopardize the legal case against Patrick Webber. Therefore, he was only able to answer four of the ten allotted questions asked – the names of the three women who accompanied the Vice President on his flight to Missoula; yes, one of the men being charged with treason was in fact the Vice President's Secret Service agent; and the tree branch stuck in the wheel well was a result of the runway being too short. Because the FBI was still investigating the role Carl played in the kidnapping, he would not provide the name of the injured man who was taken off the plane in Missoula. He could only confirm that the man's injuries were not due to gunshot wounds. The other questions the press asked all pertained to things that might be brought up at the trial.

Before concluding the briefing, the Press Secretary again assured the press the White House would be holding daily briefings on this matter.

CHAPTER 36

• • •

PATRICK WEBBER WAS IN JAIL. He was appalled when he was escorted directly off the plane in D.C. and taken to a specially convened Federal Court. The Attorney General requested he be remanded without bail and the Federal judge agreed given the seriousness of the charges. Those son-of-a-bitches are going to pay for this, he fumed. His clothes were taken from him and he was stripped searched, the most humiliating thing that ever happened to him. Clad in the orange prison garb, he now sat in his cell in a special area of the prison, away from other prisoners. He only got a few hours sleep. Every time he closed his eyes, he was consumed with hatred for the three old ladies who ruined all his plans. Thoughts of how to kill them raged through his brain. Tomorrow he would start making arrangements to have them killed.

The next day he met with his attorney, Jacob Weinstein. His anger hadn't gone away. In fact, it intensified. His eyes bore into his attorney's face. "What the hell am I paying you all this money for when you can't even get me out on bail?"

"Patrick, listen to me," Jacob said. "The government has charged you with kidnapping and on that one there is absolutely no bail. But I already have a series of motions I'll be filing later today to reduce the charge and delay the trial. I feel I can get you out of here within a few weeks."

Webber curled his lip into a snarl. "You are a lousy piece of shit as far as I'm concerned."

"Just be patient, Patrick."

"I want to see my executive assistant, Gary. Make it happen . . . today," Patrick demanded.

Jacob grimaced. "Only family members and your attorney are allowed to come here."

"I don't give a shit about the damn rules. Grease whatever palms you have to, but I want to see Gary today."

"Okay, okay, Patrick. I'll see what I can do. "

Later that afternoon, Jacob Weinstein returned to the prison accompanied by an "attorney" from his office by the name of Gary Adams. Gary had worked for Webber for eight years. He was as amoral as Webber. He had no qualms about putting people out of business, so Webber could then scoop up the remaining shell of the company for a song. In eight years he had bribed hundreds of people with either money or blackmail. He privately maintained a file of pictures of Senators, judges, high-ranking business people caught with prostitutes – female and male and young boys and girls. He considered this file his retirement fund.

When Webber was brought into the room, he told Jacob to sit at the other end of the table. He then leaned across the table as far as he could and whispered, "I want those three women killed. You can go up as high as a million. But I want it done before the trial, the sooner the better."

"Done," was all Gary replied. He knew of a Corsican he could contact. For a million dollars, he would get the best.

CHAPTER 37

• • •

BILL HAD TURNED OVER PATRICK Webber's cell phone to the FBI shortly after he landed at Andrews Air Force Base. They worked on the phone during the night.

The FBI team at Burnt Fork scoured Webber's cabin. Because of the sophisticated electronic equipment installed on the cabin roof, the team was relentless about checking every inch of the cabin. There was no computer on the jet still parked on the runway. The Vice President said Webber was not carrying a computer when he and Janice came upon him on his way to his plane. Therefore, if there was a computer, it still had to be in the cabin. Their search paid off. At eleven o'clock that night, they found it concealed behind a wall with an intricate hidden spring. The computer was packaged and included with the other evidence to be sent to the FBI laboratory in D.C.

By 3:39 a.m. seven boxes filled with preliminary evidence to be analyzed had arrived at Andrews Air Force Base. The cargo was brought to the FBI headquarters under armor guard. It still would be days before the Agents on the ground in Montana would be through gathering all the evidence. Yet the seven initial boxes provided a treasure trove to the FBI, especially the computer and Webber's cell phone. They were able to trace emails back and forth between Webber, a U.S. Senator, a Manager of an offshore hedge fund and a CEO of an international manufacturing company outlining the kidnapping plot. Subpoenas and warrants were issued late the next morning.

As the team of FBI agents arrived at the Senator's house in Georgetown, they discovered two squad cars and an ambulance in front of his house. When the lead agent questioned the Georgetown police detective, he learned the Senator had apparently committed suicide earlier that morning. Much to the chagrin of the Georgetown police, the FBI immediately took charge of the investigation. Upon entering the Senator's home, they found him slumped over his desk in his study. There was a bullet hole in the right side of his head and the gun, recently fired, was on the floor. There was a suicide note on the desk explaining how the Senator could not face the consequences of his part in the Vice President's kidnapping.

The FBI could not arrest the hedge fund manager either, since he fled during the night and was now residing at his offshore home on an island country in the Caribbean that did not have an extradition treaty with the United States. The Assistant Head of the FBI called his counterpart at Interpol. He requested their help in working together with a small European country that did have extradition treaties with both the United States and that Caribbean country. The FBI wanted Interpol to be able to establish whether the manager of the hedge fund broke enough laws in the small European country to cause their government to extradite the manager. Once he was extradited there, the United States would then extradite the manager back to the U.S. to stand trial for his role in the kidnapping.

The CEO of the manufacturing company had also disappeared – for now. He wasn't at his office or any of his homes in Richmond, Aspen, New York City or Palm Beach. It wasn't easy to hide. The FBI knew, given time, they would find him. They would begin surveillance of his electronic media, monitor phone calls at his home and business, and put a tail on members of his family and business associates.

• • •

Across the "Pond", an Interpol agent in London was listing to the European electronic chatter. It was near the end of his shift. It had been another boring day with only a few snippets of chatter to pass along to the researchers and field agents to pursue. He had his cup of tea raised to take a sip when he heard a strange code message coming from an Internet Café in Corsica. The agent immediately put the cup down and grabbed a pencil to mark down the exact time. When the day's tape was reviewed, the researchers needed the time in order to locate the exact message on the tape. Interpol had been tracking this email address for months, but they still hadn't been able to trace the owner, since the routing into and out of the person's server was extremely intricate. They were quite sure it belonged to an assassin for hire out of Corsica. He listened to the exchange, all in code and passed it on as "urgent" to the research staff.

Later that night, the Interpol researchers would alert the field agents who would alert the C.I.A. agent stationed at the American Embassy. They felt an assassination would be taking place on American soil in the near future. So far that's all they had gleaned from the back and forth coded messaging.

The C.I.A agent passed it on to the Washington C.I.A. office. The message did not end up at the FBI. Hence, no one associated this with Patrick Webber and the three women.

CHAPTER 38

• • •

WHILE ALL THIS WAS GOING on across the world, that afternoon the three women were finally released by the FBI in Missoula. Because the women were important witnesses and since Emily's van was still parked at the Helena Airport, a Federal Marshall drove them down to Helena. They asked to be driven to Burnt Fork Lake to retrieve their belongings and clean up any remaining food that was left. They were told the area was now off-limits.

On their drive down, Emily sat in the back seat and had a worried look on her face. "Listen, I don't want to have to face Nancy alone and not be able to tell her everything that went on. You heard her on the phone, screaming. You know what she's like. She'll drive me crazy. So how about we call our kids and tell them all to meet at my house when we get home. That way we tell them all at the same time, and you can help me defuse Nancy's ranting. To tell you the truth, I just don't have the strength to deal with her right now. I need sleep."

Both Peggy and Janice smiled. They had known Emily long enough to understand what Nancy was like. "Don't worry, Emily, We'll help you." Janice said. "Actually, I think Amy will get a kick out of the *cloak and dagger* thing."

"I agree. We will stick with you, Emily. My son, Alex, should be okay with an edited version of what happened too. He served in the Navy aboard a destroyer in the Atlantic. He knows all about keeping secrets. In fact, there are things he experienced he still can't tell me about."

Emily looked relieved. "Thanks. Let's call them now from here. Once we get to Helena and retrieve my car, we should be home around 10:00 pm tonight. They can come over then."

The Federal Marshall dropped them off at the Helena Airport and then he followed Emily's car to her house before heading back. Even though it was only 9:45 p.m. when they pulled up, they saw all three of their children sitting in their cars waiting for them.

"Here goes nothing," Emily said as she opened her garage door and pulled her car in. She hardly had her car door opened before Nancy started bombarding her with questions.

"What happened? Where have you been all this time? Why haven't you returned my phone calls?"

"Come on in and we'll tell you as much as we can," Emily said.

When they were all seated in the living room, Emily asked if anyone wanted something to drink. Thankfully, all declined. She was too exhausted to play hostess right now anyway. "Janice, why don't you tell our kids what happened?" Emily said.

Amy had a smile on her face even before her mother began her narrative. "This ought to be good," she said with a twinkle in her eye. Nancy rolled her eyes and let out a martyred sigh.

"Well, we were camping at Burnt Fork Lake and we discovered the Vice President and the pilot of the twin engine plane who had severe injuries. Because he was in no condition to fly, Emily and Peggy agreed to fly everyone out. Thank goodness for them."

Alex looked at his mother. "I watched the White House Press briefing tonight. They said Patrick Webber has been charged with kidnapping. You wouldn't know anything about that, would you?"

"We can't say any more about what happened, Alex," Peggy answered as she shrugged her shoulders.

"Oh, come on," Nancy said. "What do you mean you can't tell us more? The Vice President of the United States was kidnapped, for crying out loud."

Alex glared at Nancy. "Calm down, Nancy," Alex said. "I understand there are things that can't be said right now." He looked back at his mother. "When this is all over, you are going to tell us everything, aren't you?" Peggy along with Janice and Emily nodded their heads in agreement.

"Bill told us to be very careful when discussing this, even to our families," Janice said.

"Bill? You mean the three of you are on a first name basis with the Vice President of the United States?" Amy chuckled. Again all three women nodded their heads.

"I don't believe this," Nancy chimed in. "This is difficult for me, Mom."

Emily got up and sat next to Nancy. She put her arm around her daughter. "I know, sweetheart. But for now that's all we can tell you. Look at it this way, we're all safe and sound and back home again." Nancy leaned against her mother.

When Alex, Amy and Nancy realized they wouldn't be getting any more out of their mother's, they left. Alex and Amy drove their mothers home. None of the women could get into bed fast enough. They were so tired after what they had been through.

CHAPTER 39

• • •

HOWEVER, SLEEP WAS FITFUL FOR all three of them. At 5:00 a.m. Peggy finally gave up trying to go back to sleep for the umpteenth time and got out of bed. She decided to make a cup of coffee. It was still pitch black outside. On her way to the kitchen, she saw light filtering through the slits in her living room curtains. That's strange, she thought. The lone street light across the street never shines that bright. When she parted the curtains, she was stunned. There were numerous T.V. news vans parked in front of her house. Each had a spotlight aimed at her house. She immediately closed the curtains and then surreptitiously peeked out again.

"What the heck is going on?" she whispered. Because the women were on-route during the White House press conference yesterday, Peggy was unaware the Press Secretary had given out their names on national T.V. She got her cell phone out and called Emily.

"Are you up?" she asked when Emily answered the phone.

"I'm awake, but still in bed. I don't think I slept more then thirty minutes last night."

"Well, get up and look outside your front window. There are T.V. news cameras everywhere!" She could hear Emily moving around. "What are we going to do?" Peggy whined.

"Oh, for goodness sake. What are you talking about?" was Emily's retort on the way to her living room. "Oh my god, I just looked out. It looks like the Fourth of July out there! Have you called Janice to see if she's been invaded?"

"Not yet."

"Okay, I'll call her and call you back. We can't live like this. No, wait. I'm going to text you so the three of us can talk back and forth together."

Within three minutes, Peggy received a text from Emily.

Amy told Janice the President's Press Secretary gave our names out last night on national T.V. for crying out loud! That's why all the news people are here trying to pump us for information.

What are we going to do? Peggy shot back to her friends.

Well, we can't answer any questions. You know what Bill told us. But how can we make all these news people go away? Emily asked.

I know what we can do. Let's meet at my house for breakfast in one hour. Have the news people follow both of you to my house. Now all the T.V. people will be here in one place. Then let's go out and meet them and act as dumb

as we can so they will finally give up and leave us alone. It should be fun.
Janice was the comic of the three.

Sounds like a plan. See you at 6:15. Peggy, you in?

Yeah. See you at 6:15. I'll drive.

Peggy couldn't back out of her driveway, since a large news van was parked at the end of her driveway and the news people were very aggressive as they surrounded her car trying to ask her questions. She tried inching down to the street, but they wouldn't move. Finally in desperation, she rolled down her window and told them to follow her. She told them she and her friends would answer their questions together. The news people shot to their vans and started their motors.

The same thing happened at Emily's house when she pulled into her driveway. Again she was surrounded by reporters shouting out questions. Emily came out of her house and was immediately besieged. They swarmed. She could barely make it to Peggy's car. Peggy, once again, rolled down her window and told them to follow the two of them. Their questions would be answered by all three of them. And off the caravan went in the early dawn of the morning.

"This is worse than fighting off the bad guys at Burnt Fork, for crying out loud," Emily said.

"Look behind us," Peggy chuckled. "With us in the lead and the news vans following close behind, we look like O. J. Simpson when the police were following his white car for miles and miles."

When they got to Janice's house – the same thing. Peggy's car was stopped at the very beginning of the driveway while reporters pounced on the car. The news people who had been following them jumped out of their vans and joined the mob. Once again, Peggy rolled down her window.

"If you don't move out of my way, my friend and I aren't getting out of this car. And then our friend will not come out of her house. Therefore, you won't get any news story at all. What's it going to be, people? You standing here trying to shout questions through closed car windows, or the three of us coming out on the lawn and answering your questions?" The reporters slowly made an opening, so Peggy could pull up to Janice's garage door. Yet when they got out and were walking to the house to get Janice, they were pelted with a barrage of questions.

It wasn't even an hour since they decided to meet and Janice was already dressed to the nines – bright colorful clothing, hair combed and in place, make-up on. Of the three, she knew how to make an entrance. "Okay, we're all in agreement? We act as dumb as we can and tell the reporters nothing. I don't think we should mention Burnt Fork Lake. For sure, they will be swarming all over the place. Probably break into your cabin too, Peggy. I'm going to say I never heard of Patrick Webber. How about you guys?"

Emily nodded her head. "Okay, we give nothing away other than the fact we flew the plane with the Vice President." She walked to the door. With her hand on the knob she looked back at her friends. "We're on," she said with a smile and twinkle in her eye as she opened the door.

The horde of reporters began shouting out questions before they even had the front door closed. The women calmly walked down to the end of Janice's driveway and were surrounded by cameras and reporters with microphones shoved in their faces.

"Was the Vice President kidnapped by Patrick Webber?"

"I have no idea," Peggy answered. (True, because only Bill said he was kidnapped. Webber never told them he did it.)

"You do realize Patrick Webber has been arrested and may be charged with kidnapping?"

"Really?" Peggy said.

"Wow," Janice chimed in.

"No kidding?" Emily asked.

"Why did you fly the Vice President to the Missoula Airport if you didn't think he was in danger?"

"Because he asked us to," Emily responded. (Technically, close to the truth.)

"Where did you fly from?"

"An airstrip," Janice said.

"Where was the airstrip located?" a reporter demanded in a belligerent tone.

"In the woods."

"Who fired shots at you?"

"No one fired any shots at me," Emily said. She looked at the other two women for their reaction.

"Me neither," Peggy said.

Janice just shrugged her shoulders and shook her head. (Technically they were all telling the truth, since Bill's Agent and the steroid man shot, not at them, but at the plane.)

"Then why did one of you tell the Missoula Airport Control Tower you were being shot at?"

"Oh, that", Emily said while she waved her hand in a dismissive manner. "While we were doing our pre-flight check, I thought I heard sounds of gunshots coming from the surrounding woods. This is hunting season in Montana, you know," Emily said. (Technically true, since she couldn't see what was happening outside from the cockpit.)

"Can you explain why two of the men being charged with kidnapping are in the hospital with gunshot wounds?"

"Oh my. Are you saying the hunters in the woods shot those two men?" Emily asked. "What is this world coming to?"

"Who was the injured man taken off your plane in Missoula?"

"We found him on the way to the plane. We could see he was injured, so we loaded him on the plane, because we felt he needed to be in the hospital," Janice said. (Even though many things happened in between getting Carl out of the shed and deciding to fly the plane, technically they did find him on the way to the plane.)

"What was his name and how did he get injured?"

"First of all, we don't know how he got injured," Emily said. (True because they found him beaten, but did not see him being beaten.) She turned to her friends. "What did he say his name was . . . Claude, John, Brian?"

"No, I think he said his name was Eugene," Peggy said.

"That's it," Emily said while she snapped her fingers. "His name was Eugene." Emily gave an innocent smile as she nodded her head. (This one was a lie, because none of the women felt Carl and his family should be subjected to this pack of jackals right now.)

"We don't think you three are telling the truth. The people have a right to know, since the charge of kidnapping is being leveled against Patrick Webber," one reporter interjected.

Peggy took command of the situation. "Look, we just got home late last night and haven't had a chance to watch the news about everything that went on. This is the first time the three of us even heard of charges of kidnapping against Patrick Warner." A reporter corrected her by telling her his name was Patrick Webber not Warner. "Oh yeah, right. Patrick Webber. Good grief. We're just three old ladies, for crying out loud. Other than flying the Vice President to Missoula, we have no idea what all went on. We're sorry, but there is nothing we can possibly tell you. Isn't the White House holding daily press briefings? Why aren't you folks in Washington, D.C. getting the latest news there rather than standing here in this driveway?"

They could see the reporters were skeptical and didn't believe them, but they did cease trying to throw out any more questions. With that, the three women turned and headed back to the house.

Once inside they snickered and did a high five. They hoped their performance would be the end of being stalked by the press.

• • •

The Vice President was sitting with his family at his kitchen table having breakfast of orange juice, bacon, eggs and toast. Now that he was safe, he was famished. He had the small T.V. in the room turned on and was watching what the news channels were saying about what happened to him in Montana. The CBS newscaster broke into the program to announce they were now going live with a report from their affiliate in Helena, Montana. The three women aboard the plane with the Vice President were being interviewed.

Bill slumped in his chair and dropped his head to his chest. *Oh brother, what are those women up to now? If they say anything to jeopardize the case against Webber, I'll strangle them.* He shushed his family so he could hear what they were saying. By the end of the interview, he was chuckling.

"Good job, ladies," he whispered.

CHAPTER 40

• • •

JANICE LIVED IN A TWO-STORY house in a quiet neighborhood in Helena. The subdivision was old-fashioned in that all the neighbors knew each other and looked out for one another. The backyards of the houses on Janice's street all butted up to the backyards of the houses on the next street. One could stand on the cross street in the middle of the block and look all the way down to the next cross street, because this was Helena and not one of the home owners would even think of fencing in their back yards. That would be snooty and surely offend the neighbor across the way.

The Corsican hit man parked his car on the cross street farthest from Janice's house. It was 10:56 p.m. in late November as he began quietly walking down the utility easement between the backyards. Janice's house was located second from the corner near the other cross street. He had checked out her house earlier in the week. His plan now was to break into her house and kill her then take a few trinkets to make it look like a robbery gone bad. The problem for him was he had only gone about seventy feet, and already he was freezing cold. He was from the island of Corsica in the Mediterranean where the yearly mean temperature was 72 degrees. He was wearing a black turtleneck jersey and black sweat pants. His jacket was a black, nylon windbreaker. He had never heard of an Arctic Low. Tonight the Low had driven the temperature down to ten degrees above zero by early evening in Helena. One hand was in his jacket pocket, but the hand holding his gun with a silencer was growing numb.

Janice's neighbor, Mrs. Stimpsky, lived one door down from her. But Mrs. Stimpsky lived on the other street so it was their backyards that were kitty corner from each other. Mrs. Stimpsky had a dog named, "Muffy". She loved Muffy, Everyone in the neighborhood loved Muffy. Whenever Mrs. Stimpsky took Muffy for a walk, children in the neighborhood would gather around to give him a hug. Muffy loved hugs. His tongue would loll, his eyes would glaze over, and his short, stumpy tail would twitch. Actually, "Muffy" was a misnomer, since Muffy was a five year-old, 190 pound, male Rottweiler.

However . . . Muffy had one unusual quirk. He absolutely hated strangers. That's why Mrs. Stimpsky always made it a point to immediately introduce Muffy to any new family who moved into the neighborhood. Then he would know the new people were friends and could pet and hug him. But when a UPS person made a delivery, Mrs. Stimpsky would have to lock Muffy in the house and go out through her garage to meet the delivery person. While signing for the package, Muffy could be heard barking menacingly in the house. Delivery people never stayed around to chat.

Every night like clockwork at eleven p.m., Mrs. Stimpsky let Muffy out into the backyard so he could do his final business for the night. She never turned on the back porch light, because she didn't want to disturb her neighbors. Besides she knew dogs could see very well in the dark.

Muffy had just taken his final whiz for the night and was about to return to the house when he spotted the stranger creep passed his yard. He zeroed in on him. His ears flattened. He lowered his head and the hairs on his neck and back stood straight up. The thousands of year old wolf genes in his DNA kicked in and he slowly and quietly began to stalk the stranger who was heading for Janice's house. Just as the Corsican turned toward her house, Muffy struck. His huge jaw clamped down on the man's left arm. His teeth sank into flesh. The Corsican was left-handed and when the dog attacked he automatically dropped his gun. Then he hit the dog on the head with his right fist. Muffy let go, but gave a ferocious growl before attacking again. The man shouted, raised his arms and tried to protect his face. Muffy caught the Corsican's jacket sleeve in his mouth and shook the man's right arm so hard, the sleeve ripped at the shoulder. Then he let go and began to bark incessantly. Backyard lights began to turn on down the entire block. Mrs. Stimpsky could be heard calling Muffy. Janice looked out her patio door. She saw a man running through the backyards down to the cross street at the end of the block. Muffy stopped the chase when he heard Mrs. Stimpsky on the patio yelling for him to come back to the house.

The police were called. They found the gun in Janice's yard. But, they found no sign of the stranger or his car. No one associated the incident with Janice directly. That night all the neighbors kept their backyard lights on.

The next day after the fiasco of last night, the Corsican couldn't believe his luck was finally changing. As he was driving by Emily's house to reconnoiter, he saw her drive out of her driveway. He followed her. She drove up to another house and beeped the horn. An older lady came out and got in her car. He checked the pictures he had of the three women and saw the second lady was Peggy. He realized he could do both women at the same time. He was mollified. The sooner he got the job done, the sooner he could get out of this country. He hated the United States.

He watched as the women pulled into a mall parking lot. Even better, they parked at the end of a row which meant there would be less traffic here. They got out and walked to the entrance. There was a slot next to their car. He decided to park there and wait for them to return. When they came for their car, he would shoot them both and be done with it. Even though he dropped his gun last night, he had a second gun he brought with him from Corsica stashed underneath the front seat. He didn't want to chance anyone seeing the weapon if they passed his car.

The pain in his arm was killing him. The swelling was making it numb. Until this assignment was over, he didn't want to take any pain medication lest it mess with his concentration. "That shit dog," he muttered. Last night when he got back to his hotel room, he cleaned the jagged gash on his arm as best he could and wrapped a cold wet towel around it. He knew he needed stitches, but couldn't take the chance going for medical help. This was another reason he wanted to get out of this country. Back home there would be doctors who would fix him up and wouldn't dare ask questions, not like here where endless forms had to be filled out.

Just like not knowing about what an Arctic Low was, the Corsican had no idea there was a new craze sweeping across the country – carjacking. Gangs of teenagers were stealing cars and then taking them on joy rides until they ran out of gas. They would smoke some pot and then simply walk away from the gasless cars.

He had been sitting in his car for over an hour and was getting more frustrated by the minute. Suddenly his car was surrounded by four punks who had guns pointed at his head. They yanked the driver side door open and made him get out of the car. He didn't even have a chance to reach under the seat to get his gun. And he couldn't go for the knife strapped around his ankle. Even if he tried, his arm was almost useless now. The kids grabbed his keys and pushed him to the ground. They jumped into his car and took off laughing and flipping him the bird out the car windows as they drove away.

He got up and stood there stunned to think something like this could ever happen to someone like him. He was a professional assassin and he was powerless. He uttered an oath in Corsican – loosely translated, it meant "fuck it". Fortunately, no one saw what had happened to him. That's all he needed, some do-gooder who would call the police. He turned and stormed out of the lot on foot. He would call a taxi to drive him back to his hotel. He was through with this assignment. Even though it was a million dollars, he didn't need it. He was already rich. He would make arrangements to return to Corsica tonight. To hell with this crap.

Two minutes later Emily and Peggy came out of the mall. As they were walking to their car, neither of them had a clue about how close they had come to losing their lives.

● ● ●

Bile rose in the back of Patrick's throat when he heard about the Corsican refusing to complete the killings. That's what you get when you hire foreign help, he thought. All of them were a bunch of pansies. Now he was more determined than ever to get those three old broads. He decided to do this himself. He would approach in-mates here in the federal prison. He knew the scum here would get the job done and for a lot less money too.

CHAPTER 41

• • •

FOR THE NEXT THE NEXT six weeks the Department of Justice and the FBI worked tirelessly gathering over one hundred and thirty-nine boxes of evidence – both hard and electronic – to prove kidnapping. Speed but above all accuracy was demanded from all who worked on this case. Numerous men and women at both agencies slept in their offices for weeks and only went home for a change of clothes. No one wanted this case to drag on and on. No one wanted Patrick Webber to be able to spend even one minute out of jail. The Attorney General presented the Justice Department's case to a Federal Grand Jury. Within twenty minutes, the Jury came back with a unanimous decision stating the Justice Department had sufficient cause to bring the case of kidnapping to trial.

Patrick Webber's attorneys brought twenty-three separate petitions before the court trying to reduce the charge and delay the trial. None of them held up and the trial was set to begin during the second week of January. The Attorney General herself would be trying the case for the defense. Subpoenas were issued to eighteen witnesses. Peggy, Emily and Janice received them along with the Vice President, Secret Service Agents Krall and Daniels, Carl, and a slew of technical people from various government agencies.

Four weeks before the trial was to begin, a criminal serving twenty-five years to life for murder who was in the same Federal penitentiary as Patrick Webber requested a meeting with the warden. He said he had information about the up-and-coming kidnapping trial. He wanted a reduction in his sentence in exchange for his information. Members of the FBI and Department of Justice attended the meeting. They agreed to reduce his sentence if they felt the information was warranted. He then told them he had been approached by Webber to arrange the murder of the three women who were with the Vice President. Webber said he would pay him $100,000 if all three were killed before the second week in January.

Three things happened when the meeting was concluded. Patrick Webber was immediately moved to solitary confinement. They did not know how many inmates Webber had approached with his murder-for-hire plot. Arrangements were made to bring the three women to the Marine base located in Quantico, Virginia. And the Secret Service was informed to add additional detail around the Vice President.

This was the beginning of the Christmas season. The women did not go quietly. Kicking and screaming would be closer to the truth. One thing all three of them demanded was they wanted to tell their families about the latest development. In usual government fashion, numerous calls had to be placed to Washington before the FBI gave them permission to inform their families.

• • •

It was Christmas Eve and the women met in Emily's apartment on the Marine base. It was the first Christmas any of them ever spent without their families. They were not even allowed to make any phone calls. They hardly spoke while eating the Christmas meal of turkey, stuffing, mash potatoes and beans prepared by the cooks in the mess hall. Their three FBI guards had joined them for dinner.

Finally, Emily looked around at the sad faces of the people assembled at the table. "Nuts to this. Enough with the long faces and feeling sorry for ourselves. We've got to remember the members of our military stationed all over the world who can't be with their families at Christmas. Furthermore," she said as she nodded to their guards across the table. "These three aren't able to celebrate Christmas with their families either. They're stuck here having to babysit us. I refuse to allow a creep like Patrick Webber spoil another minute of this holiday. We have so much to be thankful for."

She raised her glass of wine. "Merry Christmas to you all. And three weeks from now, we are going to get that son-of-a-bitch who did this to us." That broke the ice. Everyone at the table chuckled and raised their glasses in the toast.

Two days later an attorney from the Justice Department came to the base to take their depositions. When he was finished, he also coached them how to act on the stand.

"Just answer the questions. Above all don't add more than what is being asked," he told them. "Anything you say beyond what I ask could open the door for Webber's defense attorney to pounce. I want you to know what to expect from him. Webber's attorney is Jacob Weinstein. He is ferocious in court, and will do everything he can to twist your answers and confuse you. His main focus will be to discredit you as a reliable witness in any way he can. Don't be afraid. You just stick to the truth and keep yourself as calm as you can. After what you three women have been through, I believe you will do just fine."

After he left, the women went back to Janice's apartment to rehash what the Justice Department attorney told them. Being kept here on the Marine base was turning out not to be so bad. Every morning at ten o'clock, a young Marine would bring them a pot of fresh hot coffee and a mid-morning snack. Today it was cranberry scones. They poured their coffee, put a scone on serving plate, and gathered around the kitchen table to discuss what they were going to do on the stand. They knew their testimony was going to be some of the most damning against Webber. This Jacob Weinstein would be attacking everything they said.

Peggy took a bite of the scone and looked at her friends. "I think I am going to be very bland when Weinstein asks me questions," she told them. "I will try very hard not to offer any more information other than just yes or no. That might throw *him* off. What do you think?' Both women nodded in agreement.

"I like that," Emily said. "Of the three of us, you're the one who can keep your emotions in check. I, on the other hand, have a much shorter fuse. Maybe I should be the one to attack him as much as he is going to attack me."

But the other two reminded her those actions might antagonize the jury.

"Rather than *attacking* him, Emily, when he asks threatening questions, why don't you roll your eyes or give him a pained look like you think his questions are dumb?" Janice suggested. "That way there won't be anything verbal he can refute."

Emily pursed her lips and slowly nodded. "That might work," she said.

Janice snapped her fingers. "What if I play the part of the "little old lady?" she asked. "That way when he attacks me he'll come off looking like a big bully. Seems to me the jury would feel sorry for me and be on my side."

Emily raised her hand. "High-five, on that one, Janice."

Peggy had her elbows on the table and her hands folded under her chin as if in prayer. She gave a quiet snort. "We're going to be eaten alive on the stand. None of us has ever been a witness before."

"Hey, look at it this way, Peggy" Emily said. "None of us had ever rescued the Vice President of the United States at two o'clock in the morning before either. We had never been shot at before. We had never flown a plane that took off the top of a tree. But we did do all of those things and we all survived. We'll get through this too."

CHAPTER 42

• • •

THE FIRST TRIAL FOR KIDNAPPING began with Patrick Webber as the only defendant, since the Justice Department felt he was the mastermind of the plot against Vice President Andersen. Right now the Attorney General wanted to get Webber behind bars as quickly as possible. The other two men, the manager of the hedge fund – now being extradited to the U.S. and the corporate CEO – who had been apprehended hiding out only two blocks from his own house -- would be tried later along with the Secret Service Agent, James Kovac, and Webber's men, John Howard and Brian Clemmons. The trial had been underway for three and a half weeks before the three women were scheduled to testify.

• • •

Frankie Hughes was a street punk in Washington D.C. whose ego was greater than his reputation. In other words, Frankie was a complete screw-up. Two weeks ago, his cousin called him from prison and told him about Patrick Webber's offer to hire a hit-man to shoot the three women testifying against him. He told Frankie, Webber would pay $20,000 for the hit and asked if Frankie would do it. Frankie was elated and readily agreed not realizing his cousin planned on keeping $80,000 of the $100,000 Webber was actually paying. He was so busy thinking about all the ways he would spend the twenty thousand dollars that he didn't hear his cousin tell him the hit had to be *before* the women testified. First, he was going to quit his nothing job. With twenty thousand dollars who needed it? Then he was going to buy a humongous big screen T.V. and a new leather jacket so he would look good while he strutted around the neighborhood. Hot dog, he thought. $20,000 was going to put him in the big time.

Frankie had a friend who was a janitor in the Federal Building. When the trial began, he paid him $200 to bring an automatic weapon and ammunition into the building. Because his friend emptied waste paper trash every day in the dumpsters outside the building service entrance, the security was more lax there than at the public entrance. His friend was able to get the gun into the building and hide it behind boxes in a store room. Frankie planned on entering the Court House through the public entrance gun free. Once in the building, he would get the gun from his friend.

Frankie watched the news to find out when the women would be testifying. His cousin told him they would be driven into the underground parking area. Therefore, he planned to be in the garage and shoot all three of them before they got on the elevator. He even practiced how he would shoot the women while standing in front of his bathroom mirror. He decided to hold his hand sideways like the actors did in the movies about street gangs. Then he pretended pulling the trigger. He would say "Pow, pow, pow" and then sneer. He thought he looked so cool.

The problem was Frankie, ever the screw-up, hated getting up early in the morning. On the day the women were to testify, instead of getting to the Court House early to get himself in position in the garage, he over slept, missed his bus, and then had trouble finding his friend to even get the gun. Consequently, he came out of the garage stairwell just as the doors of the elevator with the women and their FBI guards were closing.

There was no way he was going follow them and try to shoot them *inside* the Court House. There was no easy escape route in there. Because he didn't pay attention when his cousin told him to shoot the women before the trial, he decided to wait and get the ladies after they testified and came back down to the garage. He would merely have to run down the ramp and out of the garage to escape, and then he could collect his $20,000.

• • •

When they arrived on the 6th floor, the women were required to wait outside the courtroom until they were called. They settled down on a bench next to the door.

"Do we all understand how we're going respond to Webber's attorney?" Janice asked. "Peggy, you're going to try to give only yes or no answers. Emily, try to keep that temper under control. You just give him non-verbal eye rolls or pained facial expressions when you feel you're getting to the boiling point. And, I will try to be the sweet, little, old lady being badgered by the big, bad, defense attorney." She wiggled her eyebrows and smiled at her friends.

"Brought to you by the same sweet, little, old lady who shot two men trying to kill us," Emily chuckled.

CHAPTER 43

• • •

Peggy was the first to be called. The courtroom was packed when she entered, but she was able to spot her son with his family sitting at the end of a middle row. She smiled at him. It was so good to see him. She hoped the FBI wouldn't take her back into seclusion before she had a chance to spend some time with him. She noted her son had saved a seat for her next to him. One good thing was once she was through with her testimony, she would be able to remain in the courtroom and hear the rest of the day's testimony.

Patrick Webber turned pale when he heard Peggy's name being called as a witness. *She was supposed to be dead by now.* He leaned over to his attorney. "What's she doing here? Are all three of them here?" he hissed.

"Yeah, they are," Weinstein answered not understanding why his client was upset.

They should have been killed by now. Those three can corroborate Andersen's testimony. Without them, it would just be my testimony against his. *What the hell happened.* Webber's face was red with fury. *Everyone including this imbecile of an attorney is completely useless.*

"Don't worry, I'll take care of them on the witness stand." Weinstein blanched when he looked back at his client. "In the meantime, get the look of rage off your face before the jury sees it," he warned Webber.

After Peggy was sworn in and took a seat in the witness box, she gave a slight smile to the Vice President who was sitting at the Prosecution table. The Justice Department attorney who had taken their depositions a few weeks ago approached the witness stand. He walked her through the events that took place at Burnt Fork Lake from the time they first spotted the twin-engine plane land through their flying the Vice President into the Missoula Airport. Just like the attorney instructed, she answered the questions that were asked and did not offer further information.

Now it was attorney Weinstein's turn to question her. Only *yes or no, yes or no* was the mantra Peggy silently repeated as he approached her.

"Missus Cunes, how old are you?" Weinstein asked.

"Sixty-nine."

"Do you work out at a gym?"

"No."

"So you are sixty-nine years old. You don't work out and yet, according to your testimony, you single handedly knocked out a man who was 6 foot 4 inches tall and weighed two hundred and eighty pounds. That seems almost impossible, doesn't it?"

"No."

Weinstein seemed thrown off for a second with her terse response. He glared at Peggy and then a slight smile glinted over his face. His look seemed to say, okay, lady I'm going to get you.

"I would now like to show a video tape of an interview you had with the Montana press shortly after you returned home to Helena, Montana." Mr. Weinstein started the tape at the part where the reporter asked: *"Who was the injured man taken off your plane in Missoula?"* After Janice's answer, the next reporter asked: *"What was his name and how did he get injured?"* Emily answered that question with: "What did he say his name was . . . Claude, Clarence, Brian?" That's when Peggy said, "No, I think he said his name was Eugene."

He turned off the video. Now he had a smirk on his face. "Now Mrs. Cunes, just what was the name of the man who was taken off the plane at the Missoula Airport?"

"Carl."

"Carl?" he asked dramatically. "But on the tape you said that his name was Eugene. If his name was indeed Carl, why did you lie and say his name was Eugene? Would you like me to play the video again to help you refresh your memory?"

"No."

"In other words, Mrs. Cunes, you lied? Isn't that right."

"Yes."

"Can you tell this court why it is you lied?"

"To protect Carl who was in the hospital from the press descending on him."

"Oh, so let me get this straight. You are the type of person who thinks it is perfectly all right to tell a bald faced lie when *you deem* it necessary to protect someone.?"

"Yes."

Weinstein's smiled got even oilier.

"Since you seem able to lie so easily, how can we possibly believe anything you say in this court? If you lie with impunity, how can we be sure you won't lie now, because *you deem* the Vice President needs to be protected?" He raised an eyebrow as he glared at her.

"I'm under oath," was her only response.

He did not to pursue this line of questioning further. "Now, Mrs. Cunnes, you told the Prosecutor that Carl . . . we do agree now that his name is Carl, don't we? That Carl had been beaten. How do you know that? Did you see him being beaten? Or is this another of your convenient lies?"

Peggy did a smart thing. She turned to the jury when she answered. "His jaw was broken, his ribs were cracked and he sustained a leg injury."

"Isn't it possible that rather than being beaten, he could have sustained those injuries in a fall?"

"No."

"No? And, just why is that, Mrs. Cunes? Another lie, perhaps?"

Again she turned to the jury. Weinstein immediately walked to the jury box and fiddled with his tie trying to break their concentration. "When we were returning to our cabin after our hike, as I told you before, we met Carl and the Vice President on the path. They were surrounded by Patrick Webber and his two men. Carl was fine at that point and had not been injured. Within 15 to 20 minutes, we returned to the perimeter of Webber's cabin and hid behind a hill to spy on them. We saw the two thugs leading the Vice President and Carl from the cabin to Webber's shed. It was clear he had been severely beaten by then, because one of the men had to help Carl walk. As for the question asked about Carl falling. That's wasn't possible, because all the cabins are built well below the foothills on relatively flat land, so there was no place for him to fall that great a distance in those 20 minutes to sustain those kinds of injuries."

"Where were you standing when you saw the men come out of the cabin?"

"We were behind a small hill."

"How many feet away from the men were you as you spied on them?"

"About 50 feet."

"Are you a nurse, Mrs. Cunes?"

"No."

"A doctor?"

"No."

"Hard to believe a person with absolutely no medical background can make an assessment about a person's medical condition while peeking over a hill 50 feet away." Mr. Weinstein made a production out of looking at Peggy with pure disgust.

"Now Mrs. Cunnes can you tell the Court," Weinstein paused and then added, "honestly. . . why you decided to risk the life of the Vice President of the United States by flying him out of the area to the Missoula Airport?"

"I didn't."

"Here we go with the lies again," he shouted. "Just when are you going to tell the truth? The entire Nation saw you land the plane in Missoula, Missus Cunes. Are you now going to say none of it was true?"

"Yes."

"Yes?" he shouted. "So you are saying it wasn't you who stepped off the plane that landed in Missoula? It wasn't you whom the Vice President stated on National T.V. flew the plane?"

"I didn't decide to fly the Vice President to Missoula . . ." Peggy tried to answer.

Weinstein threw up his arms dramatically. "Lie, after lie, after lie."

Peggy looked directly at the attorney and answered in a monosyllable voice, "I didn't decide to fly him out, Emily did. Furthermore, I was the co-pilot. Therefore, technically *I* did not fly him to Missoula."

He hesitated as if he were trying to decide whether he would be able to rattle her. He had never had a witness who could stay calm under his cross examination. After a moment, he said, "I have no further questions for this witness."

"You may step down," the Judge told her. Peggy left and sat down next to her son in the courtroom.

CHAPTER 44

• • •

EMILY WAS THE NEXT WITNESS to be called. When she entered the courtroom, she spotted her daughter and son-in-law. She was happy to see her grandsons with them and that they saved a seat for her. However, Nancy, ever the worrier, looked frantic. Her hands were balled up on her lap and her jaw seemed clamped shut. Emily sighed internally. *Aw, Nancy, come on. Have some faith in your mother.*

Emily was sworn in and questioned by the prosecution the same as Peggy had been. The Prosecutor took her all the way through landing the plane in Missoula, including taking off the top of the pine tree. That caused a few chuckles from the jury.

Weinstein shuffled some papers on his table before he stood up to question her. Emily kept the look on her face as bland as she could as he approached her.

"Now Mrs. Jackson in your testimony you stated the Vice President's Secret Service Agent, James Kovac shot at your plane. Is that correct?"

"Yes."

"Let me play a tape for you of your interview with the members of the Montana press." He had the tape set at the point Emily was being questioned. The jury heard the reporter ask: *"Who fired shots at you?"*

"No one fired any shots at me," was Emily's reply.

"Then why did you tell the Missoula Airport Control Tower you were being shot at?"

"Oh, that." The jury watched the tape where Emily waved her hand in a dismissive manner. "Because while we were doing our pre-flight check, I thought I heard sounds of gunshots coming from the surrounding woods. This is hunting season in Montana, you know," Emily said.

Weinstein turned the tape off and glared at Emily. "My, my, Mrs. Jackson. Here in court you state . . . under oath that Agent Kovac shot at you. But during the press interview, you stated no one shot at you. Not only that, when the press asked about your message to the Missoula Control tower, you stated you merely *heard* gunshots which you presumed came from hunters in the area. You've given so many different versions, is it possible at your age, you may have been diagnosed as having dementia?"

Pure anger soared through Emily. Her mouth opened. She jerked in her chair and had to fight to keep herself from standing up and shouting at Weinstein.

Knowing Emily, Peggy shut her eyes and sat very still hoping Emily wouldn't lose her temper. She just had to stick to their plan. The Vice President put his elbow on the table and lowered his head with his hand on his brow.

Fortunately, the Prosecutor jumped up and defused the situation before it went any further. "Objection, your Honor. The Defense is badgering the witness."

"Sustained," the Judge replied as he stared down at the Defense Attorney. He was known to run a very tight ship and loathed theatrics in his courtroom.

Weinstein then asked in a quiet voice, "Mrs. Jackson, can you explain why you have given so many answers to the simple question regarding being shot at?"

Emily took in a deep breath of air, let it out, and rolled her shoulders. "First of all, my answer to the reporter's question of who shot at me. I answered correctly. No one shot *at me*. Mr. Kovac shot at the plane, not me. The bullet went through the right cockpit window and traveled through the cockpit and out my left side window. Fortunately for me, I had just bent down to pick something up from the floor or I would have been hit."

"Why did I tell the Missoula Control Tower that we were being shot at? Because it was also true. But given the circumstances, I didn't split hairs about it being the plane or me being shot at. As for my answer to the press -- before the three of us went outside to answer their questions, we all agreed, no way were we going to try this case in the press; ergo, I said I thought shots were fired by some hunters."

"And just when did the saga of the shots heard change to shots fired by Agent Kovac?" asked Weinstein in an exasperated voice.

Emily raised her hand as if she were stopping him. She sighed and rolled her eyes slightly. She planned on saving the big eye rolling for later. "I'm getting to that," she said calmly. "I stated Agent Kovac was the one who shot at the plane, because both Peggy and Janice who were outside going through the outside pre-flight checks saw him fire his gun and told me it was him when they came back into the plane."

"Hearsay, your Honor. I ask the testimony to be stricken from the record," Weinstein shouted.

"Your Honor," the Prosecutor chimed in. "Mrs. Jackson was in the cockpit when the bullet was fired through the windows. She heard Agent Kovac state he was in on the kidnapping while she was in the shed freeing the Vice President. Before the plane took off, all parties except Agent Kovac and one of Mr. Webber's bodyguards had been subdued. Her testimony isn't hearsay, it's sound logic."

"Overruled. The testimony stays in."

Weinstein's lips were pursed together when he came at Emily again. "Mrs. Jackson, you told the Prosecution Patrick Webber kidnapped Vice President Andersen. Is that correct?"

"Yes."

When you and your friends were peeking over a hill at Patrick Webber's cabin, who led the Vice President to the shed?"

"Webber's two bodyguards."

"So you never actually saw, Patrick Webber put Vice President Andersen into the shed?"

"No," she replied.

"Did you at any time actually hear Mr. Webber state he had kidnapped the Vice President?"

Emily gave him a huge eye roll on that one. "We didn't *hear* him say it. Finding the Vice President bound and gagged in Webber's shed at two in the morning was a clue that he did do it."

"Your Honor, Counsel requests the right to treat this witness as hostile?" Weinstein asked.

"Granted."

Emily turned to face the Judge. "Wait a minute. Hold it, your Honor. What does being treated as *hostile* mean. If you're going to accuse me of it, the least you can do is explain it?"

The Judge looked down at Emily. "You are correct, Mrs. Jackson. Being treated as hostile means that from now on you must answer the Defense Counsel's questions exactly as asked with either a yes or no and nothing more. Do you understand now?"

Emily nodded. "Yes, thank you." She looked back at Attorney Weinstein with a shrug of her shoulders, she raised her hands slightly, as if to say okay what's your question?

"Did you at any time actually hear Mr. Webber verbally state he kidnapped the Vice President?" Weinstein snapped.

"Noooo." Emily answered drawing out the no dramatically, because she couldn't add the part about what she saw in the shed.

"Your Honor," Weinstein shouted.

Emily turned to the Judge. "What?" she asked. "I'm hostile. I did just what you told me to do. I answered with a no."

The Judge was leaning on his elbow with his hand over his mouth. He seemed like he was enjoying seeing Weinstein lose his cool. However, given the gravity of this case, he said, "Keep the dramatics to a minimum, Mrs. Jackson."

"Oh," Emily replied with a sheepish look on her face.

"Move along, Counselor. You got your answer," he instructed Weinstein.

"I have no further questions for this witness," Weinstein said as he stalked back to his chair.

When Emily walked back and took her seat next to her grandsons, they both gave her a big smile and a thumbs up.

CHAPTER 45

• • •

THEN JANICE ENTERED THE COURTROOM. In her usual flair, she was dressed to the nines, not a hair out of place, and she had refreshed her lipstick while waiting in the hall. She walked down the aisle like she was on the "Red Carpet". She returned Amy's smile when she spotted her and her family. Then right before she was sworn in, she gave the Vice President a little finger wave and a smile.

When she was questioned, the Prosecutor spent time specially questioning Janice about the events when she and the Vice President met Patrick Webber on the path and then asked her to explain in detail how she shot the two men who were shooting at the plane.

Weinstein's first question when it was his turn to cross-examine was, "Missus Winters do you own a gun?"

"Oh, good heavens no," Janice replied. "I would never own a gun."

"If that's the case, then how could you possibly expect the jury to believe your Annie Oakley saga about shooting the two men?"

"I don't own a gun, but I wanted to know what guns were all about, so last Spring I took gun lessons at a shooting range. That's where I learned to shoot. I had an excellent instructor too."

"Where did you get the gun you used in Burnt Fork Lake?"

"We took it off one of Mr. Webber's beef-cakes or goons. I don't know what to call the man. How are you referring to him?" she asked Wcinstein.

"Employee will do, Missus Winters," Weinstein replied. "So when you and the Vice President went to look for Patrick Webber, you were carrying the gun?"

"No. Bill, I mean the Vice President was carrying it. And, we weren't looking for Mr. Webber. We were going to Mr. Webber's jet to rescue his other Secret Service Agent who was being held hostage. It was on the way to the jet we met Mr. Webber trying to make a run for it. I asked the Vice President for the gun so he could subdue Mr. Webber. And, that's how I got it."

"Your Honor, move to strike the testimony of reason why they met Patrick Webber. There is no basis for 'to make a run for it'."

"Agreed," the Judge replied. He instructed the jury to disregard the words 'to make a run for it'. He looked down at Janice and said, "Missus Winters, please restrict your answers to just the facts. Don't add editorial comments."

Janice blinked her eyes and quivered her chin as if she was about to cry. "Yes, your Honor," she said softly. She meekly looked back at Weinstein.

"So let me get this straight. You, who doesn't even own a gun, single-handedly held off two men shooting at the plane?" Weinstein smirked.

"Yes, that's right."

"One of the men you were shooting at was a Secret Service Agent. Isn't that right?"

Janice said, "Yes."

"In reality wasn't he shooting at you, because he didn't know who you were? And, yet in your gun crazed way, you wounded and possibly tried to kill the very man who was trying to protect the Vice President?" Weinstein shouted.

Janice paused to do the little old lady routine, tears welling up, eyes blinking and chin quivering. "I would never kill anyone," she said in a soft voice. "That's why I specifically aimed for his leg to stop him not to kill him."

"Mrs. Winters, you expect the jury to believe you were able to hone your extraordinary marksmanship to that degree after taking . . . what one or two lessons at the gun range?" he raged. "Law enforcement personnel practice for months to reach that caliber. Isn't it just pure luck no one was murdered?"

"No. I'll show you," Janice said. She raised two hands, one as if it were a gun and the other cupping the gun hand. She raised her imaginary gun to the space between Weinstein's eyes and pulled the imaginary trigger. He blinked and took a step back when she did that. "You see, if I aim for your eyes and shoot you, you would probably be dead before you hit the ground. Or if I aimed just a little lower at your heart, same thing. I would have killed you. But with those two men, I aimed my gun at their legs, like this," she said as she lowered the imaginary gun to Weinstein's upper leg. "Now do you see why I said I would never kill anyone? It's where I aimed."

"According to the medical report from the hospital that treated the two men, the Vice President's Secret Service Agent was shot in the leg and the foot. Yet Mr. Webber's employee was shot in the upper arm. So your testimony about keeping the gun aimed low was a lie, wasn't it?"

"No it wasn't," Janice answered with a sorrowful look on her face. "First of all. I shot the Agent in the leg, like I told you. He had two guns. One dropped when I hit him. Then he reached his hand down with his other hand that was holding his second gun and shot himself in the foot before that gun went flying. As far as Mr. Webber's steroid, sorry I mean employee, he was running and weaving, jumping from one bolder to another, shooting his gun off in every direction. I aimed at his shoulder to stop him, not at his heart to kill him." She had been carrying a hankie with her. She wiped her eyes with it and sniffled.

The Vice President had his head down again, but this time it was because he was trying to stifle a laugh. He knew this was an act. Janice was tougher than nails.

"That was quite a performance, Misses Jackson," Weinstein oozed. "You say you would never kill anyone while blinking back tears. Yet didn't you just tell the Prosecutor you actually held a gun under Mr. Webber's chin when you came upon him in the woods? If the gun had gone off in that position, isn't it 100 percent certain you would have killed him?"

Janice shook her head and smiled. "Oh no," she answered. "You see I didn't even have my finger on the trigger. I was holding the gun by the handle." She again used her hand as a gun and put it under her chin and tilted her head back. "You see, with the gun in this position, Mr. Webber couldn't see I was holding the gun by the handle and didn't even have my finger on the trigger. I just wanted to scare him. It worked too. Same thing when the Vice President and I walked him back to our cabin. Although I poked him in the back with the gun, again I was holding it by the handle. He couldn't see that either." She gave her head a jaunty shake.

"I have no further questions for this witness." He again stalked back to his seat.

Janice was excused and step down from the witness stand. Amy leaned over to her mother when Janice sat down next to her and whispered, "Nice touch with the hankie. I think the jury bought it." She gave her mother a wink.

CHAPTER 46

• • •

THE DEFENSE AND PROSECUTING ATTORNEYS presented their closing arguments to the jury who were then removed to deliberate. The women walked out of the courtroom with their families. The FBI agents told them they couldn't stay long because they were to be taken back to the Marine base and would remain there until the jury came in with a verdict.

"Oh, come on. Can't we even have a little time with our children?" Emily asked.

"Don't make it too long," the Agent answered.

The disappointed women hugged their children and grandchildren trying to get as much time with them as they could. They originally thought they would at least be able to have dinner with them.

"You were really brave, Mom. I can't believe you did all those things," Nancy said to Emily while blinking back tears.

Emily gave Nancy a big hug again then stepped back and smiled at her. "Thank you for saying that, Honey. It means a lot to me. I do love you."

Emily's eldest grandson rushed up to them. "Grandma, you were awesome! Wait until I tell all my friends at school about what you did. Mom, can we go? I gotta text my friend, Larry, about this as soon as we get back to the hotel."

Amy just smiled and shook her head at Janice. "I'll just say the usual – See you when you get home, Mom."

"Never again am I going anywhere without room service," Janice told her daughter.

"Wow, Mom, you were fantastic," Peggy's son said as he hugged her. "Now I can understand why you couldn't tell us everything when you first came home."

"I'm just glad none of those attorneys asked me if I was scared. I was terrified with the things we did," she whispered.

• • •

Frankie Hughes saw the women leave the courtroom. He hurried to the stairs and sped down to the first floor of the garage. When he missed his chance to shoot them this morning, he stashed his gun behind a large drainage pipe in the parking garage and went back into the building to wait. It was way too cold to remain in the garage all day. Therefore, when he came out of the stairwell, he retrieved his gun and hid between two parked cars to wait for the women to come out of the elevator.

The parking structure in the Federal building was slated for major repairs in the Spring. The cement was cracking causing deep splits in the floors on each level. Yesterday Washington had a major snow storm come through. But like most cities on the East Coast, today the Atlantic Ocean currents brought up warm air, and the snow started to melt by early morning. The areas where the cement had split open were barricaded to prevent vehicles from parking there adding to the stress. However, because of the urgency to get the garage plowed out as quickly and efficiently as possible pending Patrick Webber's big trial, last night the snow removal company plowed much of the snow in the parking lot into the barricaded slots on each floor. The removal company then planned to come back tonight and plow out and remove those piles of snow in the barricaded slots. However, by early afternoon a good amount of the snow had melted causing large puddles to form in and around those slots. The water began working its way under the piled snow to the cracks in the cement. Already the top two floors had water seeping down to the next level below.

Frankie choose a spot next to a parked vehicle to hide while he waited for the women to get off the elevator. As he was scrunched down near the outer wall, he had no idea he stood directly under one of those cracks on the second level. He was too busy thinking about the $20,000 he was going to get for the hit and how he was going to spend it. *Did he really need a leather jacket, maybe the latest phone would be better?* The melted water above was silently meandering under the piled snow and seeking its way to the crack directly above him.

CHAPTER 47

• • •

BECAUSE THE WOMEN HAD STOPPED to talk to their families for a few minutes, they reached the elevator, reserved to transport only prisoners and special witnesses, just as the Federal Marshalls were escorting Patrick Webber out of the holding area of the Court. He would also be taken down to the ground floor parking garage where a police van waited to take him back to prison to wait. He would then be brought back to the Federal building when the jury reached a verdict in his trial. The two groups met at the elevator.

"Oh, dear," said Peggy when she saw who was coming toward them.

"We'll let them take the elevator first," said the FBI Agent as he herded the women out of the way. "We'll take the elevator when it comes back up." An SUV waited on the first floor to take them back to the Marine base.

Webber just glared at the three women as he approached them. Janice made the mistake of looking into his empty eyes. Even though he was in shackles, it still un-nerved her.

The elevator doors opened and the Marshalls escorted Webber inside. When it came back up, the Agents and women entered and proceeded to the garage.

Webber's elevator arrived on the ground level. The prison van was parked and waiting on the ramp going up to the second floor. The Marshall's signaled the driver of the van that they had arrived and he could now bring the van down to the elevator level. The driver backed the van out but because of where it was parked, it had to continue up to the second floor to reach the down ramp back to the first floor.

While that was going on, the door to the elevator carrying the women opened. They stepped out and there they all were once again. The FBI Agents signaled to the driver of their SUV that was parked on the first floor ramp coming up. All the driver of the SUV had to do was back out of the space and drive up to the group.

Before the SUV driver started to back out, Frankie Hughes jumped up with his gun held sideways – just like he practiced in his bathroom mirror. "Here comes $20,000," he whispered. But, as he started to squeeze the trigger, the melted water from the second floor reached the crack in the cement and started its path downward. However, it didn't just drip down, it cascaded down right onto Frankie's head. The drenching cold water startled him and broke his concentration. Pow, pow, pow, his gun went off. But instead of hitting the three women like he practiced, the first bullet hit the opposite wall, and bullets number two and three hit Patrick Webber right in the keister. He dropped like a stone to the pavement. One of the Marshall's fell on top of him to protect him.

An FBI Agent turned to the three women and shouted, "Get down." They didn't waste a minute. They went directly to the floor. The remaining Marshalls and FBI men immediately drew their guns and fired at the car Frankie was using as a shield.

He was a screw-up, but he wasn't dumb. Frankie did not want to die. The instant he saw what had happened – the bullets hit a man not the three women, he knew it was over. He threw his gun out to the middle of the garage floor while he ducked down behind the car as bullets whizzed by. He slowly raised his hands above his head so they were showing above the trunk of the car. He was immediately rushed by the Federal agents screaming, "Get down on the floor!" The instant Frankie threw himself on the floor, he was dragged out to the middle of the floor and handcuffed with his hands behind his back. He kept repeating, "I was supposed to hit the women,"

Emily's head popped up. "What?" she shouted. She looked over at her friends on the floor. "Did you hear that guy? He just said he was supposed to shoot us! What the heck is going on?" She pulled herself to her knees and started to rise.

The FBI agent who had been watching over the women was squatted next to them. The Marshalls and the FBI were still assessing the situation. No one knew if there were more shooters. "Stay down," he ordered Emily.

"Baloney," she replied as she stood up and started to walk toward the gunman on the floor. The FBI agent made a grab for Emily, but missed. By this time Peggy and Janice were on their knees watching Emily.

It was pure chaos in the garage now. Both the FBI and Federal Marshalls were on their phones calling for back-up and an ambulance. Police sirens could be heard in the distance. The SUV and van were inching their way toward the area. It wasn't possible for Emily to reach the man on the floor. She turned around and stalked back to her friends.

"What did he mean we were supposed to be killed?" she asked.

The three friends looked at each other and then at the same time, it dawned on them. They slowly turned and looked down at Patrick Webber laying on the floor bleeding.

"You are a loser. You wanted someone to kill us, but he shot you instead," Emily scoffed at Webber.

"This is divine justice," Peggy said with a smile on her face.

"Rot in jail, you jerk," Janice added her two cents.

EPILOGUE

• • •

It took the jury only four hours to come back with a verdict of guilty. Given the severity of the kidnapping of the Vice President of the United States, Patrick Webber was sentenced to life in prison without parole. The verdict and the immediate sentencing were administered in the hospital at Webber's bedside.

• • •

Webber had been incarcerated for over two months now. On Wednesday night of week nine, he was tossing and turning in his bunk. Because of the bullet wounds received in his *tokus*, he still could not lay on his back while sleeping and still had to sit on a doughnut pillow when he was awake.

His aide, Gary, had vanished over a month ago along with one million dollars of Patrick's money. There wasn't a thing he could do about it. Once his attorney, Weinstein, was paid, he never visited him in prison again. For all the money and power and fear Webber once possessed, no one would take his phone calls any longer. None of his former backroom schemers wanted anything to do with him. Getting revenge like the old days were just pipe dreams and nothing more now.

● ● ●

On this same Wednesday evening Emily, Janice and Peggy were at the White House. Their entire families sat and watched as President Mellon honored each of the women with the Presidential Medal of Freedom for their heroic efforts rescuing the Vice President of the United States at Burnt Fork Lake.

ACKNOWLEDGEMENTS

• • •

To Daniel Gerard, Chief Flight Instructor of Spring City Aviation, for his kindness and patience to me while explaining small planes, airports, and general flying information. He was even gracious enough to review and edit the passages I wrote about when the women were flying the plane.

To my cousin Phil Kimery, as a former Forest Ranger who told me more about trees than I wanted to know, but he brought the mountain area to life.

To Phil's wife, Millie, a native Montanan who gave me the idea to set my story in Burnt Fork Lake and provided an appreciation for the state of Montana.

To my daughter, Patti, who again designed the cover of this book.

To my grandson, Tyler, who really did ask the question, "What if we are just an experiment and someone is watching us from space?"

BIOGRAPHY

• • •

JACKIE GRANGER BEGAN HER WRITING career in retirement. Before she retired she was a C.P.A. and tax accountant in the Corporate Tax Department of a large financial institution. She has traveled to 21 countries around the world. . . 19 were visited after she was 54 years old. Currently, she lives in a small town in Wisconsin to be near five of her eight grandchildren.

Made in the USA
Lexington, KY
05 July 2017